Paul was here?

He'd said he would never leave Charlotte, not even for her. But here he was, taking away what he knew she wanted more than anything. What could they have possibly offered him?

Layne moved through the rest of her day in a daze, completing her tasks by rote and skipping the Paul Waverly meet and greet that had been set up at the end of the workday.

Paul was a part of Layne's life that she had tucked into a corner of her heart and soul.

She shut the door to her apartment, kicked off her shoes, dropped her tote on the floor next to her discarded shoes and dragged herself to the living room. Her cell phone chirped. She dug in the back pocket of her jeans and pulled out the phone. Tina's smiling face lit up the screen.

Layne's voice cracked when she tried to say hello.

"Layne? What's wrong?"

"Paul. He's here in DC. He got the anchor job."

For a moment, silence hung in the air. "When was the last time you spoke to him?"

Layne sighed. "Been
like pinpricks to her h

"Well, at some point, … le
knows you're here."

"Exactly! He knows I'… …ed
this and yet—" She blew out a long breath of frustration. "You're right. We will have to talk at some point. We'll be working together." She nearly choked on the word *together*. "I'm going to have to get my head...and my heart together for the inevitable."

* * *

Dear Reader,

I was always intrigued by what happens behind the scenes of everyday environments. As a former employee of ABC Television (many moons ago), my interest in the ins and outs of programming and office shenanigans was born. Fast-forward and I had the kernel of an idea for a novel about what happens at a daytime talk/news show after the lights go down. Enter Layne Davis and Paul Waverly.

Layne and Paul are hot off-screen "secret" lovers until an opportunity presents itself to Layne, an offer she can't refuse even though it means leaving her job, her home and her lover. She is certain this opportunity will take her to heights she's dreamed of. That is, until Paul, many months later, is offered and accepts the job Layne believes was rightfully hers—and Paul knows it.

Needless to say, Layne and Paul must come to terms with who they truly are, and what they truly want, all against the backdrop of a scandal that rocks the network and their lives.

I do hope that you will simply love this sexy, fast-paced workplace romance with a twist!

Until next time,

Donna

DONNA HILL

AFTER THE LIGHTS GO DOWN

ISBN-13: 978-1-335-58171-6

After the Lights Go Down

For questions and comments about the quality of this book, please contact us at CustomerService@Harlequin.com.

Harlequin Enterprises ULC
22 Adelaide St. West, 41st Floor
Toronto, Ontario M5H 4E3, Canada
www.Harlequin.com

Printed in U.S.A.

Donna Hill began her career in 1987 writing short stories for the confession magazines. Her first novel was released in 1990, and since that time, she has more than one hundred published titles to her credit and is considered one of the early pioneers of the African American romance genre. Three of her novels have been adapted for television. She has been featured in *Essence*, the *New York Daily News*, *USA TODAY*, *Today's Black Woman* and *Black Enterprise*, among many others. Donna is a graduate of Goddard College with an MFA in creative writing and is currently in pursuit of her doctor of arts in English pedagogy and technology. She is an assistant professor of professional writing at Medgar Evers College and lives in Brooklyn, New York, with her family.

Books by Donna Hill

Harlequin Desire

After the Lights Go Down

The Grants of DC

Strictly Confidential

Harlequin Kimani Romance

The Grants of DC

What the Heart Wants
Forever Mine

Visit the Author Profile page
at Harlequin.com for more titles.

You can also find Donna Hill on Facebook,
along with other Harlequin Desire authors,
at Facebook.com/harlequindesireauthors!

Mom, I miss you every day.

One

"This is Paul Waverly for WNCC's *News at Ten*. Stay safe out there. Good night." He flashed his signature smile and the network went to commercial.

Layne sighed deeply from her cushy spot on the plush living room couch, pointed the remote at the television and turned it off. She lifted the glass of white wine to her lips and took a short sip. Pitch-perfect as always. But she would expect nothing less than perfection from Paul. He was the consummate professional. Audiences loved him. His rich brown handsomeness graced the covers of magazines across the country. His face lit up the screen every night at ten. He could go anywhere he chose in the television business. Rumor had it that he'd been courted by both ABC and NBC networks in New York, as well as cable news stations, and had turned them all down, touting that his roots were in North Carolina, not to mention that WNCC countered every offer. So, he stayed. As a result, WNCC bent over backward to give Paul Waverly whatever he wanted, including his penthouse in downtown Charlotte, an expense account and a six-figure salary.

She rose from the couch and headed to the bathroom for a hot shower. She had an early call in the morning and it was already near midnight.

After soothing her skin with her favorite body oil, she slipped into a pale peach satin gown that shimmered and reflected the light when she moved. She went back to the living room to refill her wineglass and returned to bed, just as the key clicked in the door.

Her pulse skipped the way it always did. Part of the excitement was the secrecy, and the rest was the sheer thrill.

"Hey, baby."

She set down her glass of wine on the nightstand, got up and crossed to the threshold of their bedroom. She reached up and stroked the hard line of his jaw that exhibited the slightest bit of stubble.

"You were fabulous as usual," she cooed and lifted up to kiss his lips. She clasped the lapels of his navy suit jacket, the one he'd had custom-made on a trip to Italy. His striped tie was loose, the top button of his snow-white shirt undone.

He slid his arm around her waist and pulled her close against him. "I bet you say that to all the boys," he said against her mouth before filling himself with her lips.

Paul thrilled her in places and ways that no man had ever been able to do. She moaned softly as his hands glided across the smooth satin of her gown and slid down the tiny straps, while she worked the buttons of his shirt, unfastened his belt and loosened his zipper.

Falling in love with Paul had kept her in North Carolina longer than she'd ever intended. She'd had a plan when she graduated at the top of her class from Columbia University's School of Journalism with a minor in political science. She would spend a year at a small station, build her portfolio, gain experience and then head to Washington, DC, and *The DC Morning Show*. It had been her goal since she was a teen and had watched in starstruck awe as Cynthia Medley, the first Black female anchor, stared into the camera and delivered the breaking political news of the day, interviewed some of the most prominent faces in government, and did it all with an ease and style that flowed from her with every breath she took. Her face had graced billboards and the sides of buses for more than a decade. There had been no other woman to compare with her then or since.

Layne believed from the bottom of her soul that *she* would be that new face of broadcasting.

Then she'd met Paul, the charismatic, ridiculously sexy anchor for WNCC News, crowned Charlotte's most eligible bachelor.

It had been July, her second week at the station.

She'd been in the control room, gathering up all the notes from the day, and readying the room for the next shift, when Paul walked in. They'd eyed each other in the corridors, exchanged basic pleasantries and cordial smiles, but they'd never been alone in a semi-darkened room until then.

"I've been meaning to properly introduce myself," he'd said. The brandy-smooth voice that enthralled millions now filled the space between them. Her skin had tingled as she felt the thump of her pulse in her throat. Heat flushed the shell of her ears.

He'd stepped closer and slid his hands into the pockets of his slacks, and she would have sworn that had he not, he would have stroked her bare arm.

"Paul Waverly," he'd said instead of touching her.

She was mildly disappointed that he didn't touch her and even more appalled at herself for entertaining the idea.

She'd smiled. "Layne Davis."

He'd nodded as his to-kill-for lashes slightly lowered over dark brown eyes. "I know."

She'd blinked rapidly, tilted her head to the side. "You know?"

"I try to make it my business to know who's on the team."

"Oh." She cleared her throat. "Well, it's an honor to meet you—officially."

"I've actually asked around."

She frowned in question. "Asked around?"

"To find out who you were. What you were about."

"And?"

"Let's just say I like what I've heard. But... I've never been one to take someone else's word. I like to find out things on my own—professionally and personally."

Her throat had gone dry. She was so hot she was sure she would pass out.

"I was hoping that maybe I could take you to lunch and you could tell me all about big bad New York City." He smiled that smile, and he could have asked her to walk out into traffic with her eyes closed.

Their attraction was explosive, and before she knew it, her two-year plan had turned into a four-year stint in Charlotte, North Carolina, as she worked her way through the production department until she was offered to pinch-hit minor stand-up spots covering soft local news whenever the need arose. Her hunger for an anchor spot had lessened, but it was still willing to feast if the opportunity presented itself. When it did, she would be ready.

"All I could think about was coming home to you," he was saying now, his voice raw and hungry. He lifted her in his arms as if she was a newlywed virgin, and carried her to the bed they'd shared for the past year.

Sometimes she thought that maybe he'd sprinkled some juju in her glass of wine during their first lunch together. What else could explain the mind-altering lovemaking that left her crying out for the holy trinity, shuddering and whimpering in total submission to the power he had over her body? Like now.

Like the way he wound his hips—in homage to his

Caribbean roots—when he was deep inside her, and hit and teased *the* spot, pushing her to the edge only to bring her back over and again. Shots of electricity zipped through her. She trembled. Wept. Held on.

Paul slid his hands beneath her ample rear. With a firm hold he took control of her movements as he rotated her hips against the increasing pace of his deep thrusts.

"Ohhh." She pressed her fingers into his back.

"Open for me," he whispered.

A shudder raced up her spine. She knew what was coming. Lust whipped through her.

Paul raised her thighs onto his shoulders and extended them into a wide, perfect V. He drew up on his knees. She was completely at his mercy and he at hers.

"Look at me," she urged.

Paul dipped his head to look into her eyes.

"Say it," she demanded and squeezed the muscles of her slick insides.

Paul groaned, thrust deep and hard. That was his first answer. Always.

"Yessss," Layne cried out. "Now say it," she urged and gripped him inside her again, then once more and again.

"Ahhhh!" His voice was ragged. The veins in his neck were like ropes.

She cupped her breasts that overflowed her palms and lifted them to him. "Here. Taste."

Her pink-painted toes were now reaching back toward the leather headboard as Paul continued to stroke, leaned forward and suckled and laved and suckled her offering until he was crazy drunk with her.

Tears of rapture slid from the corners of her eyes and down her cheeks. The flutters began on the soles of her feet that pointed toward the sky, down the backs of her thighs, shook her rear, coursed along her spine, shot out to her limbs and pooled in a blast of white lightning in the pit of her stomach. Whatever control she thought she had was gone. Her body became one electric charge. Her insides gasped, shuddered, gripped and released and gripped Paul's erection like a velvety wet vise.

"Say it," she cried out as pleasure roared through her.

"Ahhhhh! I love you. Oh, God. Ohhh." His back arched. Her fingers cupped him and gently squeezed. "Yesss!" He exploded, shot and exploded into her as her body conquered and captured the essence of him.

"I l-love you, too," she stammered between heaving breaths.

Spent, he collapsed on top of her. She slowly lowered her legs, locked her ankles across his thighs to keep him nestled inside her a while longer. She stroked the soft waves of his dark hair that had curled into tiny damp spirals. "I love you, too," she softly repeated.

By degrees Paul slipped out of her and rolled onto his side. He draped a protective arm across her stomach. He kissed the corner of her damp neck right above her collarbone. Just the way she loved it.

Her lids fluttered. She drew in a long, deep breath.

She had a good life. Maybe not the exact one that she'd dreamed, but she was…almost fulfilled…most of the time. She had a solid job that she enjoyed. She had friends and a man that loved her and wanted the best for her. What more could she ask for? And when the time was right, they would let everyone know that they were a couple.

She closed her eyes and began to drift off to the steady rhythm of Paul's heartbeat against her. What more could she want was the last thought that floated through her head before a satiated sleep overtook her.

Their opposite work schedules were a definite plus in keeping any rumors or suspicions about their relationship under wraps. While she spent most nights in Paul's penthouse apartment, she still maintained her one-bedroom condo for appearances. Besides, since she had to be in the studio by ten in the morning and Paul didn't need to arrive until at least three in the afternoon to prep for his ten o'clock spot, no one had connected any dots that led to them, as far as the couple knew.

"See you tonight, babe," Paul whispered, planting a soft kiss on the back of her neck.

A shimmer ran up her spine. Her lids fluttered. "Try to stay out of trouble until I see you later."

"You wound me," he teased and turned her around to face him. He gazed down into her eyes. "We won't keep us a secret much longer," he said softly. He ran a finger along her cheek. "Promise."

Layne drew in a breath and offered a tight-lipped smile. "When the time is right, the time will be right," she replied even as she wished things were different—now.

She grabbed her tote with her laptop and shoulder bag from the kitchen island counter. She gave him a quick kiss. "Later."

Layne smoothly eased her steel gray Audi—a present to herself on her thirtieth birthday—into the flow of downtown traffic. Paul wanted to buy it for her, but she'd insisted it was something she wanted to do for herself. Not to be deterred, he'd bought her a diamond bracelet and taken her away for a romantic weekend in Vail, where they were waited on hand and foot and she'd even learned to ski—a little. As much as she loved Paul, there was still something missing—not in their relationship but in her life. She was satisfied, but what she wanted was to be fulfilled, and the longer she stayed in Charlotte, the farther away her dream became.

She pulled into the underground parking lot on North Tryon in the building that the station was housed in, next to the Bank of America tower. Gathering her things, she steeled herself for another hectic, nonstop day.

If there was one thing she had to admit, it was that no day at WNCC was ever the same. There was always a constant flow of energy, and of course with the entire globe in some form of chaos from one day to the next, news was never lacking.

She rode the elevator to the tenth floor and exited onto the long, beige carpeted corridor, the walls lined with the publicity photos of the "stars" of WNCC, and the numerous renowned guests that had been in the studio over the years. Her step slowed for a moment as she came upon Paul's photo. Inwardly, she smiled. One day her face would stare out from the walls. But it wouldn't be here. That much she was pretty certain of. Her destiny was in front of her. All she had to do was figure out how to get there.

"Good morning. Good morning," she greeted as she passed the array of staff that darted up and down the corridors. She waved at her colleagues that sat in their glass offices, stopped to snatch up a bagel and a cup of freshly brewed coffee from the commissary table and continued to her office at the near end of the long hallway.

She slid her ID card along the slot and her door popped open. Within moments she'd powered up her computer, was settled behind her small and cluttered desk, stacked with folders and her to-do list on a yellow legal pad, and was sipping her cup of coffee.

Part of her responsibility, along with her intermittent reporting duties, was to schedule and confirm all guests, which often entailed cooing at and coddling handlers, whose main goal in life seemed to be to make hers just a bit more difficult. Their requests for their bosses ranged from things as benign as spring water with lemon to fully stocked limos. It was one good thing about working at a smaller station—you were able to get your feet wet in multiple areas if you showed the potential.

She dragged in a breath and reached for her desk phone just as her cell phone chirped and stopped her midway.

Layne smiled when the familiar name lit the screen.

"Hey, girl," she greeted.

"I hope you're sitting down," Tina Gerard began. Tina had opted to head straight to DC to work for the *Washington Post* after they'd both graduated from Columbia's School of Journalism. With the exorbitant cost of New York living, they'd become roommates and the best of friends. Tina had tried unsuccessfully to convince Layne to come with her to the capital, but Layne had a plan, and not even Tina's pleading and faux threats of disowning her as her bestie could change Layne's mind.

"I have about ten minutes before someone will want something," she half joked.

"You need to pack your bags, your audition tapes, your bio and get your ass on a plane, train or automobile to DC."

Layne sat straight up in her leather chair. "Say what?"

"You remember my Uncle Ernest?"

"Yes, yes, of course. Talk faster, girl," she urged, excitement flooding her voice.

"Okay, okay. Anyway, he's a board member emeritus at WWDC. You know, the freaking *Morning Show*, girl! Anyway, he still has friends there."

Layne's pulse pounded in her temples. "Tina, I swear if you don't—"

"I got you an interview! Well, my uncle arranged it, since I'm his favorite niece in the world."

The air hung for a moment in Layne's lungs, then suddenly released in a gush. "Oh. My. God. Are you serious?"

"I wouldn't play with you like that." Tina paused dramatically. "And there's more."

Layne's thoughts raced. "More?"

"The interview is only a formality. If you want the job of assistant producer…it's pretty much yours."

Layne blinked so hard and fast she could have set off the butterfly effect. "Tina…no freaking way."

"Yes, girl," Tina squealed.

Layne's eyes fluttered closed. "Oh my god. I… This is what I've been waiting for."

"Exactly. Now all you need to do is pull your stuff together, tell them folks at WNCC adios and you're at your dream station. From there it will only be a matter of time before you get that anchor spot. I just know it, girl."

"Dreams do come true," she murmured.

"You need to get here by next week. The executive producer, Deanna Mitchell, wants to meet you, give her stamp of approval before anything is finalized."

Layne's heart thumped. "Do you know her?"

"No. I hear she can be a hard-ass, but she knows her stuff. *The DC Morning Show* is number two in ratings because of her. You'd be working directly under her. That's why you need to charm her out of her Red Bottoms."

Layne's brows rose. "Hmm, fancy."

"Very. I also hear she's a clothes horse. All the latest designer everything, and doesn't take kindly to her team looking like they just got off the bus."

Her mind raced through her wardrobe. Inwardly, she cringed. "Okay. I'll make it work."

"You betta. And of course you'll stay with me. It'll be like old times!"

Layne giggled. They'd definitely put their mark on the streets of New York, club-hopping and attending film premieres, art shows, plays and restaurants galore.

"So make your arrangements and let me know what day you'll be here. I'm going to text you Deanna Mitchell's email so that you can connect."

"Oh, Tina. I can't thank you enough."

"I got you. Always. But we will definitely have to do something über-nice for Uncle Ernest."

"For sure!"

A light knock on her door halted the conversation.

"Yes," Layne called out.

Marlo, one of the other assistants, stuck her head in. "Needed up front," she said, almost apologetically.

"Thanks. Be right there."

She returned to her call. "Listen, I have to go. I'll call you tonight. And… Tina…love you, girl."

"Right back atcha. And congrats."

Layne disconnected the call, closed her eyes, sat back for a moment and bathed in a moment of pure, unadulterated joy. Then her moment of euphoria burst. Her eyes flew open.

What about her and Paul?

Paul slid behind the wheel of his white Tesla. At the press of a button, the electronic dash housed on an iPad-like panel lit up. The engineless machine glided soundlessly into traffic, catching the admiring gazes of passersby.

For the most part, he didn't go for flash. Too much of his life was already on blast every night across the state. The Tesla was all part of the persona that the network wanted him to maintain. And of course giving a nod to Elon Musk didn't hurt. However, what he projected on the screen was a far cry from the man he really was, or at least believed himself to be. Of course he had ambition and he enjoyed the fame and the perks of the job, but if he had his way, he'd spend his days writing the political thriller that had been running around in his head for the past couple of years. He'd travel more, maybe get a house on the beach, and he'd marry Layne. His lips flickered with a smile.

Growing up the way he had, witnessing the love between his parents and the love they showered on him and his brother he hoped to have the same one day. But the demands of his career had put hearth and home on the back burner. He had time only for the briefest of relationships. Most women that interested him couldn't handle the demands of his job and his often ridiculous hours, and as a result they lasted a month or maybe two, which had only earned him the monikers of "Charlotte's most eligible bachelor" and "ladies' man."

What he wanted was what his parents had, and he'd never thought it was in the cards for him until he met Layne. It was that kind of crazy-at-first-sight thing. Not love, but definitely I-want-to-get-to-know-you-like-right-now vibe. The downside to that instant attraction was staying under the radar at the station. It took more work to keep it a secret than to maintain it.

He made a right turn onto Aberdeen Avenue, pushed out a breath of anticipation. All that was about to change.

He'd taken his cue from Joe Scarborough and Mika Brzezinski of MSNBC, the hosts of *Morning Joe*. They were an on-screen team for years, had finally tied the knot and remained as tight as ever. They made it work. He and Layne would as well.

Everything was set. He pulled into the parking lot of his local gym, grabbed his gym bag and got out. While he walked across the lot to the entrance, he tapped in Layne's number. She picked up on the third ring, sounded rushed and harried as she usually did while at work.

"Hey, baby," he said. "I know you're busy. I made dinner plans for us tonight. It's been a minute since we've had a night out." The truth was they couldn't risk being seen in a candlelit restaurant or any other intimate setting as long as things remained as they were between them at work. When they did go out together it was generally on trips out of town, out of the limelight. Tonight would be different.

"Really?" she said, her voice rising in delighted surprise, mixed with apprehension.

"Yes, really. Great food, wine, maybe some dancing."

She giggled. "What brought all this on? We usually have to plan our getaways like secret agents," she half joked.

"It's Saturday, I'm off and I want to spend the night out with my woman," he crooned.

She pushed out a breath. "Fine by me. I get off at six. And… I have some news to share…over a bottle of wine."

"Can't wait. I'll see you at home. Reservations are for eight."

"I love you, Paul," she whispered.

"Love you right back." He disconnected the call and pulled open the heavy glass doors to the gym. A good workout would definitely unravel the ropes of nerves that wrapped around his insides.

Layne pressed her phone to her chest and tugged on her bottom lip with her teeth. Timing was everything, she mused as she walked toward the control room. Being out together in a great restaurant would provide the perfect atmosphere to spring her news on Paul.

Since she'd spoken with Tina, her head had been swimming, first in pure ecstasy and then in flashes of dread. As promised, Tina had sent over Deanna's contact information and Layne was scheduled to meet with the executive producer next Wednesday. *The DC Morning Show* was arranging her flight and accommodations. Everything was moving at lightning speed, after having stalled for years. What would it mean for her and Paul? How could they make it work? Long-distance relationships were difficult under the best of circumstances, but couple that with demanding jobs and unreasonable hours…and she didn't want to think about that now. She pulled open the door to the control room. The blue-green lights from consoles and computer screens always gave the control room an ethereal feeling.

She crossed the industrial-gray carpeted floor, inching behind the thick leather seats occupied by the directors and producers of *Live with Tess*, the third-best afternoon cooking show on network television. Tess Hampton was no Rachael Ray, but she had a strong following and her audience share was growing.

"Mike." She leaned down and whispered in the assistant director's ear. "Feed these to Tess during commercial." She placed three large index cards next to his keyboard.

Mike glanced up and gave a short nod. "We'll get them on the teleprompter. Another Harold Morgan request, I presume," he snarked with a half grin.

Harold Morgan was the station president, and he frequently inserted himself into the show with last-minute one-liners praising some celebrity or politician that he'd discovered liked a particular dish or fine wine. He'd brought on Tess two years earlier, and rumor had it that he was more than her mentor, which didn't make life easy for Tess. No matter how hard she worked, or how good she actually was, there was always the presumption that Harold had a hand in it. All the more reason why she and Paul had religiously kept their relationship under wraps.

"I'm only the messenger," she said, giving his meaty shoulder a light squeeze.

She walked back toward her office, but was stopped in the corridor by Linda Kreps, the producer for *Midday Charlotte*.

"Just who I was looking for. I was heading to your office," Linda said. Linda Kreps was like the dictionary picture of the harried, intense television producer. She was barely five foot five, with choppy blond hair that always looked like she'd been in a fight, and sky blue eyes that were magnified behind her glasses. She never wore makeup, and it was rumored that her closet only had one outfit: khaki slacks and safari shirts. On the opposite end, her partner could easily be a runway model. Guess there was someone for everyone.

"What's up?" Layne asked as they continued side by side down the hallway.

"The Carolina Arts Foundation Gala is happening tomorrow night, and I want you to cover it."

Did she look as shocked as she felt? "Really?"

"Yes, really. I think it will be the perfect opportunity for you to rub elbows with the right people and put you front and center with the honchos here at the station."

"Wow. Um. Thank you." She swallowed. Why

now? Just when her shot in Washington was at her fingertips, a new door at WNCC was opening. Those events were peppered with philanthropists, artists, entertainment celebrities and politicians. Landing interviews with just the right person…

"Problem?"

Layne blinked. "No. Not at all. Just trying to figure out what to wear." She smiled brightly.

Linda gave Layne's arm a light squeeze. "Good. Stop by my office before you leave and my assistant will give you all the information and your press pass. Ron is slated as the cameraman." They stopped in front of Layne's office door. "Oh, and you get a plus-one. I'm sure you have someone tucked away." She winked and hurried away in the opposite direction.

For several moments Layne stood stock-still in front of her closed office door. She drew in a breath and slowly released it. This day had been full of surprises. What next?

Two

While they dressed they fussed over their outfits, and argued about who took the longest in the shower. Layne applied the finishing touch to her makeup, cheerily followed Paul down to the underground parking and slid into the comfort of his midnight blue Lexus, which he'd decided was less conspicuous than the Tesla if they wanted to keep a relative low profile.

As they'd prepared for their first evening out in much too long, they'd promised each other that they would hold on to their good news until dessert.

Layne had to admit she was more nervous than excited at this point. During the ride to the restaurant she stole furtive glances at Paul's handsome profile. Even seated, his six-foot-two frame cut an imposing figure: The charcoal gray of his suit jacket spread firmly across broad shoulders, the platinum watch sparkled at his left wrist, and the dove gray silk shirt open at the collar projected the picture of a man who understood classy and cool. She loved him. There was no doubt about that, but as she considered the reality of what her future held, uncertainty about the stability of their relationship pooled in her soul.

Paul always touted that his roots, his career, his tight-knit family, friends and Layne were in Charlotte and he had no intention of changing that. So much so that she'd ceased talking about her dream to sit in the anchor's chair in DC. For Paul, travel for work and extended vacations were one thing, but relocating was not in his deck of cards, at least not any time in the foreseeable future.

Layne laced her fingers tightly together. Could they make long-distance work?

Paul was chewing on his bottom lip as he held the steering wheel in a death grip. Sure signs that he had something heavy on his mind. Layne couldn't begin to imagine what it was, but Paul had given no indication that what he wanted to talk with her about was something awful. If anything, he seemed super excited, at least until they'd gotten in the car. When the car doors shut behind them the tension grew in waves. He was uncharacteristically nervous. A feeling she'd never connect to Paul Waverly.

"Everything okay?" she asked. She placed a hand on his thigh.

He gave her a brief look and a tight smile. "Absolutely. Why?"

"It looks like you want to cut the oxygen off the

steering wheel," she said with a hint of laughter in her voice.

Paul chuckled. "No, I'm good. Just looking forward to us being out tonight—as a couple." He glanced at her again, took her hand from his thigh, brought it to his lips and placed a soft kiss on her knuckles.

Layne settled back against the plush leather of her seat. She pulled in a slow, meditative breath. *Everything will be fine*, she silently chanted. *Everything will be fine.*

When they stopped in front of the elegant, smoked-glass doors, Layne's step faltered as she actually noticed the restaurant's name etched in gold letters on the one-way windows. Guests could see out, but those on the street could not see inside. Pierre's, one of the city's exclusive French restaurants. There were times when reservations for dinner had to be made a month ahead. Clearly, Paul had planned this well in advance. Her heart thumped. *Could it be?*

The doorman dressed in all black with gold buttons on his jacket opened the door. "Welcome to Pierre's. Enjoy your evening."

"Thank you," Paul said with a short nod. He stood to the side to let Layne enter first.

The cool, dimly lit confines of Pierre's screamed elegance, from the circular tables covered in fine white linen, centerpieces of candles and lilies set in glass bowls, the gleam of silver, the hush of footsteps atop a thick red carpet, to the grand chandeliers that gave off just the right amount of illumination. Layne fought to keep her mouth from dropping open and gawking like a tourist.

Paul kept his hand at the small of her back, guiding her to the hostess's podium.

"Good evening. Welcome to Pierre's. Your table is ready, Mr. Waverly," the hostess said in an accent that was a practiced mixture of something foreign and right-around-the-corner native. Layne inwardly smiled. Mastering a universal vocal effect was part of the skill set in on-air journalism. The notion that in order to fit in one must look, behave, sound and dress the part could be exhausting. She'd love to be a fly on the wall when the young hostess was simply hanging out with her girlfriends.

The young hostess lifted her slim hand and a waiter appeared. "Table 11, Arnold." She handed him two menus and the wine and liqueur list, before he led them away.

As they were being ushered to what turned out to be a private banquette, Layne was mildly relieved that they did not cross paths with anyone they knew. But the hostess had addressed Paul by name without him saying a word, which was indication enough that they could be easily recognized. However, she was moderately soothed by the belief that anyone able to get a seat at Pierre's would be above spreading gossip. But then again…

The banquette was positioned so that the six-foot-high horseshoe-shaped leather partition faced the interior of the restaurant, with the seating tucked behind it overlooking the street. The setup gave the couple a high degree of privacy from other guests, while offering them the entertainment of life passing by on the streets of Charlotte from their coveted spot behind the one-way glass window.

Arnold placed the menus on the linen-topped table, then tucked his hands behind his back as the couple settled in their seats.

"My name is Arnold Stevens. I will be your personal waiter for the evening."

A young woman appeared by Arnold's side. "This is Michelle. She will take your drink and appetizer orders. I will return shortly to go over the entrées." He gave a single-lined smile and whirled away.

Layne kind of wanted to laugh. This was all so shi shi foo foo. She felt as if she'd been transported to an episode of *The Gilded Age* for the twenty-first century. But it was still so cool.

"Whatever you want," Paul said as he scanned the drink menu.

She smiled at Michelle. "Let's start with a bottle of Terlato."

Paul's right brow lifted in agreement. "A pinot grigio. One of the best. I've been waiting to try it."

Michelle nodded. "I can get your wine now while you decide on an appetizer, if you wish."

"That would be fine. Thank you," Paul said.

Once Michelle was gone, Paul took a deep breath, leaned forward and covered Layne's hands with his. "So, what do you think?" he asked with a glimmer of mischief in his eyes.

Layne tilted her head to the side. "I think that if you wanted to impress me, you have," she said with a delighted smile.

Paul ran his tongue along his bottom lip. "Did I tell you how absolutely stunning you look tonight?" he whispered, sounding almost awed.

Layne flushed from head to toe. When Paul looked at her like that, with a combination of love and raw hunger, her insides lit up like fireworks. She'd wanted to look extra special tonight and had taken meticulous care in choosing just the right dress and accessories. Her sleeveless, deep royal blue satin cocktail dress with its double-layered, elegantly flared skirting flowed like a halo above her knees. The boatneck with its V cut added an extra bit of dramatic detail. Her right wrist sparkled with the diamond bracelet Paul had given her, which she'd paired with tiny diamond studs in her ears.

Layne shielded her eyes with a lowering of her lashes. "No," she said softly, "but do feel free." She glanced up, locked eyes with him and smiled with invitation.

Michelle returned with the bottle of wine, opened it and poured the delectable liquid into each glass. She glanced from one to the other. "Hors d'oeuvre?"

Paul looked to Layne.

"I'd love to try the Gougeres," Layne said.

"And, um, a plate of salmon rillettes. That comes with the miniature toast, yes?" Paul asked.

Michelle smiled. "Yes, it does. I'll put your orders in. Arnold will be around to take your dinner order." She whisked away.

Paul held up his glass. Layne raised hers. "To us. To our night. To our future."

Layne swallowed. She tapped her glass against

his. "To us," she whispered before taking a sip of her wine. If Paul's plan was what she was beginning to believe it was, she wasn't sure how the evening would turn out.

She played a variety of scenarios in her mind as they went through the appetizers and mouthwatering entrée, and now the dessert had arrived.

Layne's heart had slowly begun to beat harder and faster as the evening progressed. She laughed at all of Paul's corny jokes, listened intently to his analysis of the current war overseas and the politics surrounding it, and his longing to make time to write his book.

"One of these days," he said on a sigh. He cleared his throat. "I, uh, know we promised to wait to share our news until after dessert." His gaze jumped from Layne's face to the table and back again. "I know I'm not the most romantic guy you could be dealing with and I know all this secrecy has been hard on you. But I want you to know—" his smooth baritone hitched "—that I love you. I want to spend the rest of my life with you."

Layne could barely breathe. Her pulse pounded and she swore her vision clouded over. When she looked down at the table, Paul had a tiny red velvet box sitting open on his palm, displaying a ring with a stunning sapphire surrounded by sparkling diamonds on a platinum band.

The air stuck in her chest. She covered her gasp with her palm.

"Marry me, Layne. Let's do this thing…together." He reached for her hand without waiting for an answer and slid the ring onto her finger.

Tears filled her eyes. “Paul.” Her voice cracked.

“I hope those are happy tears, babe.”

She sniffed, studied the brilliant stones on her finger that picked up the chandelier light and set off tiny rainbows around her hand. She blinked and blinked to stem the water building in her eyes. “Yes,” she finally managed. Her head swam.

“I think we can probably make an announcement at least to HR this week.”

Layne cleared her throat. “That makes sense.” She nodded as she spoke. “Then we can take it from there with the staff.”

Paul took both her hands and brought them to his lips. “I love you,” he whispered. “We’re going to be the happiest couple on the planet and I can’t wait to start our life together.” He kissed her hands, stared into her eyes. “Now, what is your big news?”

She swallowed the knot that was building in her throat. Her stomach fluttered. “Well,” she said on a breath, “I have two things to tell you.”

“Hold that thought.” He signaled for Arnold, who arrived with the speed of a ninja.

“Yes, Mr. Waverly.”

“My...*fiancée* and I are celebrating.” He threw Layne a smoldering look. “Can we get a bottle of your best champagne?”

“Right away.”

“Happy?” Paul whispered, leaning toward Layne and brushing his thumb across the stones on her left hand.

“Very,” she said, her voice slightly tremulous. “A little overwhelmed, but happy.”

"You've dealt with the constraints of our relationship from the beginning, without complaint."

"Well…sometimes," she said with a smile.

"True." He chuckled, then his expression and tone grew serious. "All of that is going to change. You can finally give up your condo and move in with me." His dark brown eyes moved across her face.

Her right brow hitched. "Give up my condo?" Even though she spent most nights at Paul's penthouse, the condo was hers, bought with her own money, decorated and furnished by her. When she walked through its doors there was a sense and level of satisfaction that she didn't feel at Paul's place.

"Of course. We'll live at the penthouse until we get a house of our own. Why would you keep the condo?"

"Because it's *mine*," she said with a bit more bite than she intended.

The waiter returned with the bottle of champagne, uncorked it with a flourish and filled two new flutes. He shoved the opened bottle into a bucket of ice. "Enjoy." He hurried away.

Paul gave a nod, then reached for his glass. "Tonight is a night for surprises and celebrations. And I want to hear your news," he said, seeming to have dismissed what she'd said.

She blinked slowly before lifting her glass as well. "Yes, it is." She tapped her glass with his and took a sip. The faint bubbles tickled her nose. She pushed aside the tense moment. *Not tonight*. "Actually, I have two pieces of news."

Paul beamed. "Let's hear it." He took a sip of champagne.

"Well," she began on a breath, "Linda Kreps came to me today and said they want me to cover the Carolina Arts Foundation Gala tomorrow night!" She almost squealed out the words but remembered where she was.

Paul's eyes widened. "What? Baby, that is major. The elbows that you will rub." His grin lit up the space around them. "Proud of you. Well deserved."

"Thank you. *And…* I get a plus-one," she said with a wink.

He tipped his head to the side, left brow arched. "Hmm, and who are you planning on taking to this shindig?"

"Well," she said on a whisper and leaned in. "There is this incredibly handsome, intelligent, funny, wildly sexy guy who makes my toes curl when he makes love to me…" She ran the tip of her tongue across her bottom lip. "I was thinking of asking him to come," she said seductively. She watched his throat bob.

"This wildly sexy, handsome, intelligent guy got a name?"

She leaned in further and beckoned him closer with a crook of her finger. She whispered deep into his ear before easing back into her seat.

Paul's jaw flexed. His hot gaze never left Layne's face as he lifted his arm to signal for the waiter and the check.

"To hell with dessert," he murmured.

Her other news could wait until morning, she decided, as she curled her body next to his while they waited for his car to be brought around. She glanced down at the twinkling ring on her finger. Her heart thumped. She hugged Paul tighter. It was what she'd wanted, what Paul had promised. She could bring up DC later. For reasons that she couldn't quite name, the thought of telling Paul about it had her nerves on edge.

On Sunday mornings they'd fallen into the cozy habit of sleeping late, reading the papers in bed and ordering a lavish breakfast from their favorite Spanish restaurant, followed by slow, easy lovemaking and an old movie.

Layne rested her head on Paul's chest. The steady beat of his heart always soothed her. Its rhythm synced with her own and there was a unique harmony that they created.

She studied the ring on her finger, still a bit dazzled by the idea that this was real. She was engaged to the man she loved. He'd done everything he'd promised. He wanted to build a life for the two of them. Maybe giving up her condo wasn't so bad. Her pulse quickened. If she got the job, which Tina assured her was in the bag, she'd have to give it up anyway. She tugged on her bottom lip with her teeth. Her stomach knotted.

"You okay?" He angled his head to try to look down at her.

"Sure. Why?"

"Hmm." He turned the paper to the next page. "Your body just got all tense or something for a minute."

"No, I'm fine," she said. She shut her eyes. It was true—at times she and Paul could read each other's bodies like maps, sense mood changes with no more than a subtle look. It was one of the many things she loved about being a couple with him. It was as if there actually was a soul connection, which was why she knew she couldn't hold on to her news about DC much longer. He'd soon feel it on her skin and in every move that she made.

She flipped the sheet off, sat up and swung her feet to the floor. "I'm going to get some more juice. Want some?"

He peered above the top of the paper, then slowly lowered it to reveal a brimming smile as his gaze settled on her naked body.

"Only if you promise to bring it back dressed just like that."

"One-track mind." She tossed her bra at him that was hanging by a strap on the end of the bed. He caught it in one hand, barely moving.

"Can't help it when it comes to you." He winked.

She snatched up his discarded shirt from the night before and slipped it on, or rather swam in it, and padded out to the kitchen. She braced her palms on the granite countertop and looked around without focusing on any of the gleaming appliances. *Can't put if off forever.* She had to be in DC for her meeting next week.

She turned to pull open the left side of the double-door stainless steel refrigerator and reached for the container of orange juice. She filled two glasses, returned the carton to the shelf and walked back to the bedroom. She placed Paul's glass on his nightstand.

"Thanks, babe," he murmured.

Sitting down on the side of the bed, she ran the tip of her finger across his hairline. "Need to talk with you about something. Actually, it's the other half of the news I wanted to tell you last night." She put on a smile.

He placed the paper on his lap. "Yes!" He sat up, pulled her close. "Let me hear all about it, wife-to-be." He lifted her left hand and kissed it.

She swallowed. "Well, you'll never guess who called me yesterday."

His brow creased for an instant. "Not a clue," he said with amusement.

"Tina. You know my friend Tina from DC."

"Yeah, sure."

Layne shifted. "You know I've always talked about wanting to be on *The DC Morning Show*." She felt the shift in the room. Paul's smile dimmed. "Well, her uncle is on the board and there's an opening and she got me in to see the executive producer. There's a position open that would be perfect for me." She said it all in a rush even as she intentionally withheld the tiny fact that the job was hers and all she had to do was say yes.

Paul's eyes cinched a bit at the corners as if the morning light was suddenly too much. "Okaaaay," he said slowly. "And you're going?" he asked as if the only answer could be "no."

"Yes. I am."

He pursed his lips a moment. He shifted his body and released her hand. "Why?"

That wasn't the question she expected. "Why?"

"Yes. Why are you going through the motions?"

She blinked in amazement. "Paul. This is something I've been working my entire career to achieve. The least I can do is hear what they have to say. I *want* to hear what they have to say," she added.

"To what end, Layne? If they offer you the job, are you seriously considering leaving?" His voice elevated in disbelief.

"What if they did?"

"That's only half of the equation. What would your answer be is the real question."

Her heart thumped. She straightened her shoulders and stood. She looked down into his pointed stare. "I'd take it."

All the air whooshed out of the room.

Paul flopped back against the down-filled pillows and looked at her in incredulity. "You're serious."

"Yes, I am."

"And what about us? I just proposed to you…last night. *That's* what you said you wanted."

"Why can't I have both?"

He tossed his head back and laughed without humor. "Both! How in the hell is that supposed to work, Layne, with me here and you in DC? For two years we had to keep our relationship under wraps. That was strain enough—on both of us, by the way. And just when we can officially get our life in order you want to add long-distance marriage to the mix? Is that what you're telling me?"

"We can make it work, Paul."

He stood so abruptly she had to take a step back to avoid being mowed over. He stalked across the room, snatched up his boxers and pulled them on, grabbed his sweatpants and T-shirt from a side chair. He turned to her, his expression a confluence of disbelief, hurt and anger. He dragged in a long breath. "Take the meeting. See what they have to say. We can talk about it when you get back." He turned to the en suite bathroom. "I'm going to get dressed and go for a run."

Even though the door barely closed, the sound of it shutting reverberated in her chest. She closed her eyes and began to mindlessly pick up their discarded clothes that had been tossed to every corner of the room the night before. They'd literally tumbled off the private elevator that opened into his expansive living room, and been so heated in their eagerness for each other that the enormous bedroom resembled the whirlwind of passion that whipped between them from one end of the room to the other and finally onto the king-size bed.

Layne picked up Paul's suit jacket and slacks and placed them in the bin for the dry cleaner. She shrugged out of his shirt and added it to the pile.

Paul emerged from the bathroom fully dressed in his running clothes. He gave her nude body a brief, hot longing look before heading to the door. "Be back in an hour or so…maybe longer."

Layne watched him go. She fingered the jewel of promise on her left hand and the sensation of uncertainty was back in the pit of her stomach.

It had been nearly two weeks since she'd set foot in her apartment. The stuffiness overwhelmed her. She dropped her carry-all on the floor of the short foyer and went from room to room opening windows. She plopped down in an overstuffed paisley side chair that faced the high windows. Late-afternoon sun streamed across the hardwood floors. She watched the tiny particles of dust dance in the beams of light. The sheer, off-white drapes fluttered ever so softly. Leaning her head back against the embrace of the cushion, she closed her eyes.

She'd straightened up Paul's bedroom, tossed the containers of breakfast food in the trash, packed up her basic belongings while Paul was on his run, took a look around and left. A little space was what was needed. If not, she felt certain things would be said that couldn't be taken back.

If Paul was this unsettled by a simple announcement about her taking a meeting for a job, how would he react when she told him she would accept the job? He'd already voiced his doubts that long-distance could ever be a thing for them.

She released a breath, opened her eyes and pushed up from her seat. Cleaning always cleared her head, and her space could use it.

Two hours later, showered, nestled in her comfy, oversize nightshirt and curled on the couch with a glass of wine at her side in her sparkling condo, Layne took a moment to reflect on her next steps.

She sipped her wine once, then again. The bottom line was, she was going to the meeting. If what Tina said was true and the job was hers for the taking, she sure as hell was going to take it. This had been her dream for years. Paul knew this. He'd known it when they met. If he wasn't willing to compromise…well… She looked at the sparkler on her finger. Just well…

Her stomach grumbled and she realized she hadn't shopped for groceries in weeks. She placed her wine-glass on the end table and leaned toward the coffee table for her laptop. Since she had a feeling she was going to be spending some time in her own abode, she was going to need some supplies.

After logging onto her favorite supermarket, she put in her order to restock her fridge, freezer and pantry. Estimated delivery was two hours. She checked the time. It was nearing four. She hadn't heard a word from Paul. She knew good and well he was back from his run. He had to realize that she hadn't just gone for a walk. She checked her cell phone. No missed call. No text. She sighed and tossed the phone to the far end of her couch.

Fine. Just like she needed some time and some space, he probably did, too. She'd let him have it. If nothing else Paul was reasonable. His training as a journalist afforded him the skills of being organized in thought and remaining objective to issues presented, which allowed him to make rational, impassive decisions. He would think this through, weigh the pros and cons and come to realize that it was doable. She had to believe that.

"Saturday was the big night, bro. You finally pop the question?" Eric asked before taking a swallow from his bottle of beer. "That ring was boring a hole in your pocket for weeks." He stretched out his long legs and looked at his younger brother. "But by the look on your face I'd think she said no. What's up?"

Paul settled back against the lounge chair and looked out onto the waning evening from their spot on the deck of Eric's suburban home.

"Yeah, I asked. She said yes."

"That's good news, right? So why the long face?" He reached over and squeezed his brother's forearm. "What gives?" He took another swallow. "Too early for cold feet." Eric chuckled, but stilled when he saw his brother's brooding expression.

Paul exhaled, then launched into the conversation he and Layne had had earlier, his voice rising and falling.

"Hmm. So…what's gonna happen if she gets the job in DC? You plan on relocating?"

"My life is here. My family. My *career.* One that I've spent the last fifteen years building…and it's set to take another major leap," he murmured too low for his brother to hear.

Eric pursed his lips and lowered his head in thought. "You might not want to hear this, bro, but Layne has career goals, too. You knew that going in."

"She has a career. Here! One that she's damned good at and she has the opportunity to grab even more of it after the foundation event."

"So basically she should be satisfied even if she's always wanted more?"

Paul shot his brother a look. "When I made up my mind to ask Layne to marry me, I saw us like Mom and Dad. Like you and Tricia. Partners. Together. For the long haul. Not some long-distance arrangement.

When would we see each other? Once a month, if that. What about a family? How the hell would that work?"

"It would work if you decided to make it work," Eric said quietly. "Listen, I get it. For all the fancy life that you live in front of the camera, at the heart of you, you're just an old-fashioned kinda guy. And that's cool. Don't get me wrong, but sometimes we have to make adjustments and they're not always comfortable."

Paul slowly shook his head. "I…can't see it."

"Is it really because you can't or you're too stubborn and you won't?"

Paul brought the mouth of the beer bottle to his lips, tipped his head back and took a long, thoughtful swallow. That was a damned good question, and if there was any way for him and Layne to figure this out, he'd have to come up with an answer.

"There's something else," Paul finally said.

Eric angled his head. "More? I'm listening."

"It's all been hush-hush. The ink on the contract isn't even dry yet."

Eric's brow rose in question. "Bruh, skip the intrigue and get to the finale."

"Earlier this afternoon, I signed a letter of agreement to host my own news show."

"Say what?" Eric sat up straight.

"Yep." He nodded and tried unsuccessfully to act cool.

"Bruh! You was supposed to lead with this. Damn, congratulations! This is major."

Paul bobbed his head and chuckled. "Yeah, man, it really is."

"Layne know?"

He shook his head.

"Why not?"

"This may sound silly but I actually didn't believe it would really happen. I mean, that's part of the reason." He placed the beer bottle on the circular wrought iron table between them. He leaned forward, rested his arms on his thighs and linked his fingers together. "It's been in the works for months but all lips were sealed. If it had gotten out, the sponsors would've bailed."

"Couldn't even tell Layne?" Eric asked, still incredulous.

"You know that for a news man who deals in facts and data, I'm a little superstitious. Truly did not want to jinx it by saying anything to anyone. Not even Layne. Once I was assured by the station president that it was definitely a done deal I knew I could ask her to marry me. I knew that even if anyone raised an eyebrow at us, they wouldn't rock the boat because of all the firepower behind the new program." He sighed heavily. "Mine was the last signature needed to seal it up tight. I'd planned to take Layne to Miami for the weekend and tell her before the station makes a formal announcement in two weeks. Sweeps."

"Wow," Eric said on a breath. "That does complicate things. For real. I mean, how *could* you leave now?"

"That's just it. I can't."

"Hey, once you tell Layne, there's no way she'd ask you to pick up and move to DC. She'll stay here. You two will get married and live happily ever after."

Paul didn't respond. He wished he could be that sure. When he'd come back from his run Sunday morning and found her gone, he knew this was not going to be a walk in the park. What would he do if she took that job in DC? They both needed some space. A few days apart were probably for the best. She'd go to the gala, make the trip to Washington, and when she got back, he'd share his news and they'd pick up where they'd left off.

"So, this new gig have a name yet? And what about your ten o'clock slot?"

Paul exhaled. "My ten will stay the same. My new gig is going to start once per month to build ratings then move to weekly. *News Hour with Paul Waverly.*"

"I am actually impressed." Eric chuckled. "You. Are. The. Man!"

They fist-bumped.

Their two-ships-passing-in-the-night schedules had their benefits, but Layne wished they would run into each other in the hall, the control room, at a meeting or the commissary. At the very least they'd have to acknowledge the other's existence, which would open the conversation door. They were both stubborn in their own way, and it would take a minute before either of them made the first move.

Usually, if they had a disagreement, they would go to their "respective corners" until something random happened: Their favorite show would come on television, or one of them would forget that they weren't on speaking terms and rush into the apartment excited about a play or a jazz event coming to town, or they'd both be reading the same news article and start talking over each other in excitement.

This was different, though. She'd actually packed a bag with the intention of…of what? Never coming back? That was ridiculous, of course. She fingered her engagement ring.

She leaned toward the mirror and coated her lashes with several swipes of mascara, reached for her lipstick and evenly covered her lips in a hot red that lit up the undertones of her skin. She'd intricately twisted her thick, naturally curly hair into an elaborate bun on top of her head. She patted the sides and tucked one of the twisted strands back in place.

Turning from the mirror, she crossed the floor to the bed, where her dress for the evening was stretched out and waiting. She shrugged out of her robe and stepped into the sequined, one-shoulder-neckline, knee-length silver dress with a center split and draped sleeve. The dress hugged her body from breasts to knees and shimmered ever so subtly when she moved.

Layne stepped into her toe-out heels and picked up her clutch. The intercom buzzed.

She pressed the talk button. "Yes, Victor."

"There's a Mr. Ron Harrison in the lobby."

"Yes. Thank you. Tell him I'll be right down."

In case it got chilly, she decided to take her shawl, so featherlight it was almost translucent. She draped it over her arm and checked her clutch for keys, phone, lipstick and compact. One good thing about the tech age was that as a reporter you didn't have to carry around a lot of equipment. All you needed was a smartphone. She took one last admiring look in the mirror. Paul didn't know what he was missing.

Layne wasn't certain what she'd expected when she walked into the ballroom. To say that she was stunned was an understatement. Photos of these events, even the live broadcasts, did the assemblage and all the accoutrements no justice whatsoever.

"Wow," she uttered under her breath, and wished that Paul was here to share this moment with her.

Ron was at her side. He'd ditched his usual body-hugging T-shirt, jeans and the latest Nikes for a pretty slick-looking midnight blue suit, open-collar sky blue shirt and spit shine shoes. He'd even combed his shaggy blond hair so that it didn't sweep across his blue eyes. If one squinted he might be able to pass for a Brad Pitt stand-in.

"So this is that whole above-our-pay-grade kinda shindig," he said with just a hint of a soft Southern note, just enough to let you know he was from here, but he'd been around, too. He adjusted the cylindrical black bag on his shoulder that held the tripod, mics and electric cords.

Layne giggled. "It certainly is." But she believed in her heart that it would not always be this way; the little girl with her face pressed up against the window of the finest toy store wouldn't be kept out of the store forever. She'd get the shiny thing in the window. Tonight she'd been given a key—it was still stiff in the lock, but she planned to turn it, and next—DC would offer her any toy she wanted.

"Let's get settled. Linda gave me a list of who she

wants interviewed and who to get sound bites from. We'll do a few stand-ups, cover as many as we can without becoming pains in the asses."

They walked side by side, weaving between the glitz and glamour, the murmur of cultured voices at the perfect decibel, the drip-drip of diamonds, the scent of perfumes and colognes that cost more than it took to feed a family.

Three enormous crystal chandeliers glistened and captured the array of colors from below and cast them about like rainbows. The take-your-breath-away windows spanned an entire wall and rose from floor to ceiling, offering an enchanted view of the skyline and the blanket of stars that sprinkled the heavens.

"Doubt it," Ron said. "Folks like this love to 'have something to say' and see their face on the screen. You've been in the editing room. Half of what we get we can't use, 'cause folks talk too much about themselves and not the question at hand."

"Hmm, that's true to a point. I mean as news people we have an agenda as well."

Ron shrugged. "I'm going to set up over there on the left. Good vantage point and lighting for your stand-ups."

"Great. I'm going to find our table."

She wound her way around the room and nearly tripped over her own feet when she spotted the entourage at the company table. WNCC had bought a table of course, but what made her heart race was who sat at the table. Holding court was Harold Morgan, the president of the network, surrounded by the executives and their spouses and none other than Tess Hampton seated to his right and his wife at his left.

Well, just damn. She brightened her smile and moved to the group.

"Good evening, everyone." She cast her gaze around the assemblage.

"Ah, Layne. Welcome," Harold greeted. "I'm sure you know everyone."

"Yes."

Stanley Martin, the senior VP and only Black male in an upper management position, stood and helped her into her seat.

"Thank you," she said, glancing up at him over her shoulder. She placed her purse on the table.

The waiters came around and refilled wine and water glasses and served an array of appetizers—lobster bisque, mixed green salad, pâté on tiny crackers, and crabmeat on beds of lettuce.

Stanley leaned over and whispered. "If these are the appetizers I guess we won't be eating the usual dried chicken."

Layne giggled. "Clearly, the foundation is using its money well," she replied.

"I've seen some of your work," he continued. He reached for his wineglass and took a sip.

"Oh." She raised an inquiring brow. "Is that a good thing or not?" She held her wineglass to her lips and sipped.

"I think you have enormous potential." He smiled. "That's why I suggested to Harold that it should be you to cover this event."

Good home training kept her from sputtering all

over his Tom Ford tuxedo. She blinked, swallowed and cleared her throat. She placed her glass on the table.

"*You* suggested?"

"Yes. Why does that surprise you?"

Did he just move closer? "I was not aware that you could pick me out of a lineup of two," she said, trying to regain her wits. He was staring at her, staring at her in a way that wasn't simply conversational and his stare held her rooted in place. She wanted more wine but she was sure that her hands were shaking.

Stanley tilted his head to the side and smiled a bit, then he rattled off her résumé as smoothly as if it was his own. Then he tossed in trivia about some of the stories she'd covered and even what some of her coworkers thought of her.

As she listened, she wasn't sure if she should be flattered or terrified. If he knew all of that, did he know about her and Paul as well? She'd opted against wearing her sparkler. There was no need to stir the pot before she and Paul worked out what they needed to work out. Equally important, why was Stanley doing all of this intel on her?

"The bottom line is," he said, lowering his voice to a whisper, "there are barely a handful of us in this business. If there is any way that I can add to that number or push someone forward, then that's what I'm going to do." He paused and seemed to move closer. "I can be a very strong ally."

"I see." She licked her lips.

"Tonight is your night to prove that my recommendation wasn't wrong." He eased back, lifted his glass in salute and finished off the contents of the flute. “You should stop by my office maybe one day next week.” His attention was taken away from her by a tap on his shoulder from the woman on his right.

Layne was thankful for the reprieve. Her pulse raced. There were so many rabbit holes she could dive into with what had just happened. On the one hand Stanley came across as the laser-focused executive who had done his homework on someone he believed was worth grooming. On the other hand, it wasn’t so much what he said. It was the tone, the insinuations, the look in his eyes, the closeness of his body next to hers.

As she numbly made her way through the entrée, she was happy that Paul wasn’t her plus-one. Who knows what would have transpired. She offered nods and small talk when appropriate, until she was finally able to get back across the room to Ron.

“Hey,” she greeted. “Did you get any food?”

“Oh, yeah. Bunch of camera folks got set up in one of the smaller rooms down the corridor. Pretty damned good, too.” He smiled and then it slowly faded. “You okay?”

She glanced at him quickly. “Yes. I’m fine. Guess I’m just a bit anxious is all.”

“You got this.” He gave her an encouraging smile. “Ready whenever you are.”

After she banished the shakiness from her voice, the rest of the evening, the interviews, the on-the-fly commentaries and the stand-ups went off without a hitch. She did her live shot for the eleven o’clock news with the chairperson of the foundation as well as a collage of sound bites from numerous guests and honorees.

* * *

"If I don't get out of these heels I'm going to scream," Layne said as she plopped down into one of the padded chairs while Ron packed up. "I just might scream anyway," she said laughing.

"Helluva night. You were great."

"Teamwork. Couldn't have done it without you. Your cues, your ability to spot the next great shot..." She pushed out a breath. "I see why you were chosen for this one."

He gave her a crooked smile. "Thanks. Means a lot."

She slowly pushed to her feet. "I hope we get to work together again."

"Yeah, me, too."

Part of her meant what she'd told Ron. The other part knew that if the vibe she was getting from Stanley Martin was any indication of what was ahead for her at WNCC and at what cost, her days at the network were numbered and she'd soon have a 202 area code—as long as things went well on her interview.

The flight from Charlotte, North Carolina, to Washington, DC, was quick and uneventful. As excited as she was about what lay ahead, part of her spirit was back in Charlotte. She and Paul had yet to really talk since she'd returned to her own apartment. Their brief phone conversations were all superficial as if no one dared to bring up the elephant in the room. He'd called her before she boarded the plane and wished her good luck, but she was sure his heart wasn't in it. She'd wanted to tell him about Stanley Martin and the vibe she'd gotten, but knew that it would only add fuel to the fire. She ended the call by reminding him that she loved him and they'd talk when she returned. He shared the same sentiment before the line went hollow.

As promised, Tina met her at the airport baggage claim area.

"Girl, girl! It is so good to see you," she bubbled, wrapping Layne in a tight hug.

"You, too, sis. It's been way too long."

"You have bags?"

"Nope, just my carry-on," she said, indicating the roller bag at her feet.

"Cool, then let's blow this joint. I'm starved. We'll drop off your stuff at my place, then get some lunch. I'll give you all the details and you will spill the beans on the foundation gala! Girl, we saw clips here. You were amazing."

Layne's cheeks heated. "Thanks. It was something."

"Um...*something*? What am I hearing?" They pushed through the revolving doors. "I parked in the lot. This way," she said hooking her arm through Layne's.

"Let's just say I need to unpack it over food and drink."

"Say no more."

They hurried toward the parking lot. During the half-hour drive to Tina's apartment, the two friends talked over, between and through each other, recasting characters and stories from their recollections from college and the many parties they'd attended, both swearing that their versions of people, places and events were accurate.

"For two highly trained and educated journalists we sure have a helluva time getting our own facts straight!" Tina said over their laughter as they pulled into the underground parking garage at Essex House.

Layne pulled her bag from the trunk and followed Tina down a short corridor and through heavy double doors to the main lobby.

"I usually just take the elevator up to my floor but I wanted to give you the fifty-cent tour first."

They stepped out into a lobby that resembled the layout of many of the high-priced hotels, with its marble floors, gleaming glass tables, mood lighting and lush seating. To the left was the on-site restaurant, and on the right, a state-of-the-art gym complete with trainers.

"So wait, you live in a hotel?" Layne asked in confusion as she took in the spaces.

Tina laughed. "No, silly. Everything on the ground floor—restaurant, gym, day care, business center—is for all of the residents. The apartments are from the second to eighth floor. There's also a roof deck that is open in the summer for private parties."

"Wow."

They walked toward the elevator.

"I had no idea. When you said you moved last year I didn't picture this."

Tina laughed. "Neither did I when I heard a couple of years ago that there were plans to rebuild this part of DC. Montgomery Grant—"

"The real estate developer!" Layne cut in.

"Yep. He pulled this all together. Him and his now wife, Lexington. She handled the design. The community center just opened across the street about six weeks ago. Plans are in the works for a major supermarket also."

"Totally impressive." From the moment they'd arrived and walked into the lobby, she felt something special and saw something even more special. Everywhere that she turned, she saw faces that looked like hers—from the staff to the guests, to residents.

"Grant is trying to single-handedly revitalize this area of DC. He uses only minority labor and vendors and the housing is actually affordable. For decades the buildings and the community in general were just left to disintegrate. It was dangerous, between the drugs and the muggings." She shook her head. "Now there is new life flowing through these streets. And wait until you check out the menu at the restaurant. His brother Alonzo Grant is the one that cooks for all the celebrities. He oversees the menu here."

"Get out! I've seen him on television."

Tina laughed. The elevator doors slid open. "Welcome to DC."

"So you think this Martin guy was trying to come on to you?" Tina asked before taking a bite of her salmon salad.

"I don't know. That's what it felt like. It wasn't even so much what he said, but the vibe he gave off. You know." She reached for her glass of iced tea. "I mean, I'm probably reading more into it than necessary with my own personal stuff being all messy. It could all be nothing, but it left me feeling kinda shaky."

"I hear ya," Tina said thoughtfully. "Well, my advice is to steer clear. And if you do go to his office, the door stays open or someone else is in there with you. No late-night meetings—"

Layne held up her hand. "I know the drill." She slowly shook her head. "It's a damn shame that these are the circumstances that we work under—still in this day and age."

"Girl, some things never change, just the outfits."

Layne snorted a laugh. "You got that right."

"There's an Olympic-sized, heated pool if you want to swim later on," she added matter-of-factly.

Layne grinned. "The beat just keeps going on."

The two friends high-fived.

WWDC television studios and headquarters were located in a fifteen-story eco-friendly structure located in Georgetown.

When the elevator doors swooshed open to the administrative offices on the tenth floor, a young woman in an arresting lavender blouse rose from behind a glossy glass-and-chrome horseshoe-shaped desk.

"Welcome to WWDC."

Layne approached. "I have an appointment with Ms. Deanna Mitchell."

"Yes, you are Ms. Davis. She's expecting you."

She reached for the phone, touched a button. "Ms. Davis is here," she said softly into the receiver. "Yes." She glanced up. "I'll walk you back."

They stopped in front of a frosted glass door. The young woman tapped lightly.

"Yes, yes, come in," came a sharp voice from the other side of the door.

Layne suddenly took on an extra level of nervousness.

The young woman pushed the door open and stepped aside to let her pass.

"Ms. Mitchell," Layne was saying with an outstretched hand as she crossed from the door to the desk.

Deanna rose to her feet in what felt like a film in slow motion. Every breath, movement, flicker of the eye was deliberate. She reminded Layne of a young Jane Fonda.

Deanna swept her wide, red-framed cat-eye glasses from the bridge of her flawless nose and placed them on the desk. "Ms. Davis." She shook Layne's hand. "Please have a seat. We're so happy that you were able to come in." The voice was in perfect modulation.

Layne shrugged out of her lightweight three-quarter coat and draped it across the arm of the chair and then sat. She placed her tote on her lap.

"How was your trip?" Deanna linked her long fingers together, the red of her nails matching the color of her lips.

"It was fine. Thank you."

"So," Deanna breathed. "I've already heard wonderful things about you. I've seen you on-screen once or twice, but why don't you tell me about yourself and why you think you would be a good fit here at WWDC." She leveled her mint green eyes on Layne.

Layne drew in a settling breath and clasped her fingers together. “I grew up…”

Deanna leaned back and tilted her head slightly to the side as Layne took her on a brief tour of the highlights of her life, education and the trajectory of her career.

Deanna offered a shadow of a smile when Layne finished. “You clearly have the education and experience.” She paused. “So many rising journalists begin their careers in smaller markets.” She pressed the tip of her finger to her lip. “Some never make it out. And that’s perfectly fine, of course. But at a major network—” she paused “—it’s different. The level of work and expectations are much higher. Our news programs are syndicated. As you know, the news position that we have open on *The DC Morning Show* requires extreme flexibility. The person in the spot must be prepared at the drop of a hat to cover a scene, prepare their own notes, pull a team together. And there may be, on the very rare occasion, the need to fill in for one of the anchors. Everyone has to be on their A game. Not some days. Every day.”

“Of course.” Why did she feel as if she’d somehow already fallen down on the job?

Deanna dragged in a breath and pushed to her feet. “I hope you’ve planned to stay through the day. I’d like for you to meet some of the staff and take a tour of the studio, and of course I’d like to review your tapes.”

Layne’s heart thumped. “Yes, I’d planned to stay through tomorrow. I’ll be heading back on Saturday morning.”

Deanna nodded. “Good.” She came from around the desk. “You can leave your things here if you like. I’ll take you around.”

“Sure.” Layne got up. She left her coat but hooked the strap of her tote on her shoulder and followed Deanna out.

Layne was beyond thrilled to walk the corridors and through the studio where the dream of her future bloomed. She smiled and nodded and tried to remember names and faces but the excited pulse beating in her temples made everything fuzzy around the edges.

When the tour concluded Deanna took Layne to lunch but for the life of her she couldn’t remember what she ordered or what she ate. The only thing on her mind was that at some point, either today or tomorrow, Monday at the latest, she was going to be offered the job of a lifetime.

“I know we offered to put you in a hotel,” Deanna was saying as they returned to her office.

“Yes, that was really thoughtful, but I’m staying with a college friend. It’s giving us a chance to catch up.”

Deanna nodded. “Yes, Tina.”

Layne’s stomach lurched. Deanna’s lips barely moved when she said Tina’s name, almost as if it pained her.

“I generally do the scouting for new talent on my team,” she said, turning her body halfway from Layne. She angled her head in Layne direction. “When recommendations come from elsewhere…” Without finishing her sentence, she moved to sit behind her desk.

Layne's smile wobbled a bit around the edges.

"In any event, it was absolutely wonderful to meet you in person. I am going to review your tapes, talk it over with a few people and we'll get back to you."

Layne licked her lips. "Of course." She lifted her jacket from the arm of the chair and adjusted the strap of her tote onto her shoulder. She extended her hand, which Deanna shook.

"We'll be in touch," the executive producer said.

"I look forward to hearing from you and thank you for meeting with me, and the tour." Layne beamed a genuine smile.

Deanna inclined her head like Queen Elizabeth from the throne and Layne knew she was being dismissed.

"So, tell me everything?" Tina said as she and Layne sipped margaritas at Tina's favorite Mexican restaurant.

Layne ran her tongue along the rim of the salted glass, then took a sip of her strawberry margarita. "Well, Deanna… Hard to put my finger on it. One minute she's warm and encouraging and in a blink cold and distant. I got the feeling by the end that she was actually ticked off that she had to meet with me, that I wasn't *her* pick."

"Hmm," Tina mused. "Even so, you have everything that they're looking for. Period. Whether she found you on Craigslist or if someone over her head recommended you, it doesn't matter."

Layne snorted a laugh. "Craigslist? Really?"

Tina shrugged. "You know what I mean."

Layne lifted a nacho chip and scooped it full with guacamole. She took a big, satisfying bite and chewed softly, running over the events of the day in her mind. "I know I can do great work. I feel it. This is where I belong," she insisted.

"I know that and you know that." She waited a beat. "What are you going to do about you and Paul?"

"Not much I can do until I get the official offer."

"Don't get cute. You know exactly what I mean, Layne."

Layne blew out a breath from between pursed lips. "We are going to work it out. I have to believe that. Paul loves me and I know that as difficult as it might be to be apart, he wants the best for me. He wants me to be happy."

"Okaaaay." She swirled a nacho chip around in the salsa and plopped it in her mouth. "Have you two spoken…like at all?"

Layne fingered the ring that she'd put back on. "Not really," she murmured. "But we will. When I get back."

Tina had gone into work. She said she'd be home about seven and promised they would have one more girls' night before Layne returned to Charlotte in the morning.

It was nearly 10 a.m. on Friday when Layne's cell phone rang. It was the Human Resources rep at WWDC calling with an offer. Layne squeezed her eyes shut, pressed her lips into a tight line to keep from screaming and listened to the HR rep go on about forms and signatures, all of which would be sent via email for her review and signature.

"As this is Friday, we would need your response in two business days, meaning we'd need to have your response by Tuesday."

"Of course," Layne managed between spinning in circles and doing the happy dance. "Tuesday is certainly doable."

"Let me just verify your email."

Layne confirmed her email. "Thank you. I'll keep an eye out for the email. Have a good day."

She let out a whoop and squeezed the phone to her chest. "I did it! Damn it, I did it." She plopped down with a thump on Tina's couch and kicked her legs in the air. Suddenly, her throat clenched and burned, and tears sprung to her eyes, a combination of utter happiness laced with terror on where her life was going—and if Paul was going with her.

Three

Three years later
Washington, DC

Layne unhooked her clip-on microphone from between the two pearl buttons on her pale peach blouse and handed it off to her technical assistant, Cherie Farmer. Cherie had been more of her right hand than a tech assistant. She was a wizard with sound and lighting, and under Cherie's expert control, Layne always looked and sounded great—even in the middle of whirlwinds of Mother Nature or at the site of screaming fire engines and whirring helicopters. To add to her repertoire of talent she handled the camera as well. Layne and Cherie together were the envy of WWDC.

"Thanks, Cherie," Layne said as she stepped into the studio van that was parked outside the Great Mall. It was the weekend of the National Book Festival and any author and publisher worth their words in print was in attendance. Some of the biggest names in the industry, National Book Award winners, Pulitzer Prize winners, the *New York Times*, *Washington Post* and *USA TODAY* bestselling authors and, of course, throngs of readers spanned across the mall for as far as the eye could see.

Layne had landed exclusive sit-downs with Mia Hunter, recently minted *New York Times* number one bestselling author, and Antoinette London, the most recent recipient of the National Book Award. The fact that both of them were women and that three of the five names on the Pulitzer short list were also women was the angle that Layne was going for in her segment.

"It's going to be a fantastic segment," Cherie was saying as she wrapped up wires and returned microphones into padded boxes.

Layne grinned and lowered herself onto the bench against the far wall. "I think we got some pretty good reactions from the crowd as well." She kicked off her shoes and flexed her toes. "We are the dream team," Layne exclaimed.

The two women fist-bumped.

Cherie sat next to Layne. "I really want to thank you for always asking for me for your projects. It has made a major difference in my career and how I'm viewed at the station."

"You deserve all the flowers, sis. You have crazy skills. From day one, when we worked together on that grand opening of the shopping center that Montgomery Grant spearheaded, I knew I wanted to work with you. I can do what I do because I know you have my back."

"Always." Cherie pushed out a breath. "Do you want to sit in on the edits when we get back to the studio?"

"Sure. The live shots that streamed earlier will need to be clipped for the news cycles."

"I'm sure a spot will air on Monday on *The DC Morning Show*."

"Yep."

"You've produced so much content for that program," Cherie said. "They really need to give you more time behind the desk."

"It's coming." Layne smiled. "Rumor has it that Brett Conway is in some trouble. If it's true he would need to be replaced as anchor."

Cherie's eyes widened. "I'd been hearing things for a while, but Brett always seems to slither out from under everything." She gave a little shiver. "So…you think you'd be in the running?"

Layne slowly nodded. "We've been doing great work. Our segment on the homeless crisis got an Emmy nomination. That's major." She blew out a breath and linked her fingers together. "It's what I've been working toward for a long time." She gripped Cherie's hand. "And when I get there, I'm taking you with me. That's a promise."

* * *

Layne sat curled on her couch, finishing off a fettuccine Alfredo and a mixed green salad while the news played in the background. Her piece on the book festival was the opening tease and had aired for a full five minutes after the commercial. Viewers were encouraged to visit the website for the full interviews and all the highlights of the event.

Layne lifted her glass of iced tea in salute. It was a great segment. She exhaled a sigh. In the background of all her shots at the festival was the outline of the Capitol Building, the White House in the distance and the Washington Monument. She remembered all too well traveling to DC to stand out on that lawn on the coldest damn day she'd ever experienced in her life to watch the inauguration of President Obama. If she ever had any doubts about getting to DC, they'd blown away with the frigid air of that January morning. That was where she belonged. With the midterm elections approaching, she was going to pitch hard to Deanna to put her out there. She'd proven she could do hard and soft news and get the interviewee to say what she needed them to say. From there, she knew an anchor seat was only a sweeps season away.

She pointed the remote at the smart TV and scrolled to the YouTube news clips from WNCC. Her heart thumped when Paul's handsome face filled the screen and the smile that had melted her heart entered the homes of millions. She listened to the smooth cadence of his baritone and remembered how that voice would whisper in her ear.

Three years seemed like a lifetime ago since they'd said their final goodbyes. Paul had said he understood that moving to DC was something she had to do for herself. He understood, he'd insisted, and he wanted her to be happy. *But…* There was always a *but. But* he also knew what he wanted for himself, and the career he'd built for well over a decade was rooted in Charlotte. She knew that, he'd pointed out. Knew it when they first started dating, knew it when their relationship progressed from sometimes to all the time, from like to love, from behind closed doors to an engagement ring for all the world to see. *But…*even though she'd said more times than he could count that she wanted their life together, when what she wanted was finally hers, she'd decided to throw it all away.

Layne squeezed her eyes shut and leaned back against the headrest of the couch. As much as she understood Paul's disappointment and unfounded feelings of betrayal, it still hurt. A hurt that trailed her during the day and moved through her dreams at night.

She and Paul were two focused, determined, career-driven people. That was part of the passion that had drawn them together, and the very thing that had ultimately torn them apart. While they might have been traveling on parallel paths, they'd finally come to a fork in the road.

They'd tried the long-distance thing for about four months following Layne's departure from Charlotte. But between Paul's schedule and Layne getting settled into her unpredictable on-call assignments, getting together had become impossible. The "I'm sorry, not this weekend," had turned to a mantra until it became clear that they were in a no-win situation. But she saw the look in his eyes, the way he barely touched her on the rare times they saw each other, the left-handed remarks about her "coming up in the world." He resented that she'd walked away from their life together, no matter how much he claimed to understand, but he had too much pride to say otherwise. Ultimately, over an hour on FaceTime, they'd agreed that it was over.

But that didn't keep Layne for longing for him, missing him, wanting him and wondering if he still felt the same way, even a little bit. She'd substituted nonstop work and going after her goals to fill all the spaces left empty by Paul, and when she finally claimed her seat at the anchor desk, all of the sacrifices would be worthwhile.

She might not have a life with Paul, but she had a good life. That would be enough. For now.

When Layne arrived at the studio on Monday morning, there was a decided buzz that seemed to electrify the air. Staff huddled in small groups murmuring and gesticulating, their words mostly too low-key to make out. She caught only a few as she hurried down the corridor to her office. *Deanna. Scandal. Anchor. Messy. About time.*

She spotted Cherie coming out of the restroom.

"Hey. What's going on?" Layne urged in a tight whisper.

"Girl. The mess done hit the proverbial fan," she said, almost giddy.

Layne's eyes widened. She hooked her arm through Cherie's. "You're killing me. What's up?" She unlocked her office door and they walked in. Cherie closed the door behind them.

"Word on the street is Deanna is replacing Brett Conway, girl. Security walked him out about an hour ago."

"Say what?"

"Yep." She nodded. "Apparently, charges were brought against him and the board couldn't shield him anymore."

Layne plopped down in her leather chair. She dropped her tote on top of the desk. "He's out," she murmured, her mind racing.

"There's an emergency staff meeting in an hour. The notice should be in your email."

Layne powered up her desktop, waited, tapped in her password and went straight to her email account. Her eyes raced over Deanna Mitchell's missive.

She sat back and let out a woof of air. Then a slow smile moved across her polished lips. Her heart thumped. Thumped. "This is my shot, C. I'm the most likely replacement. No one on the *Morning Show* has my background or experience. I've been in front of and behind the camera. This is it," she whispered.

Cherie came over and perched on the edge of Layne's desk. "You got this," she said with a beaming smile.

"*We* got this."

* * *

Once *The DC Morning Show* wrapped for the morning and segued to *News at Noon*, the staff and crew of the *Morning Show* assembled in the main conference room. Everyone was whispering behind their hands. Layne and Cherie took seats in the back of the room, the better place to get the lay of the land, and Layne wanted to relish the moment she'd be called to the front of the room when Deanna announced her as Brett's replacement.

"Thank you all for coming," Deanna began. She was flanked on either side by the head of HR and an assistant. "As you all saw or heard, Brett Conway, who has been with this network for nearly ten years, was dismissed today." She lifted her cleft chin. "He'd become the face of *The DC Morning Show*. It was as a result of his work at the network that the show was propelled to number two in its market time slot." She cleared her throat. "But his success, his years of service to this network cannot override the serious allegations that have been leveled against him. We take them seriously. And after months of an internal investigation, we have determined the allegations were true. I won't get into details as there will of course be litigation and the parties involved will not be named."

"Parties," Cherie whispered to Layne.

Layne made a moue.

"As a result, there will be some major changes to the show." The tight, stricken look on her face softened and her mouth curved ever so slightly. "I am happy, thrilled actually, to announce Brett's replacement."

Layne shifted nervously in her seat. Cherie squeezed her hand.

The HR assistant went to the door and opened it.

"Please welcome our new anchor for *The DC Morning Show*, Mr. Paul Waverly."

Layne froze. Her ears started to ring. Heat rushed through her veins, clouding her vision. Her mouth opened but no words came out.

"What the hell," Cherie hissed. She flashed Layne a look of disbelief and gripped her arm. "Layne, I'm so sorry."

She couldn't speak.

Paul was talking but Layne couldn't hear anything he was saying. The room seemed to move in and out and she thought she was going to be sick.

"I...gotta go," she said, her voice choked. She slipped out the back door and darted down the hall to the restroom.

Standing in front of the mirror, she stared at her reflection. She braced her hands on the edge of the sink and drew in long shaky breaths. How could this be happening? Paul? Here? He'd said he would *never* leave Charlotte, not even for her. But here he was, taking away what he knew she wanted more than anything. What could they have possibly offered him?

Tears pooled in her eyes and dripped down on her knuckles.

Layne moved through the rest of her day in a daze,

completing her tasks by rote and skipping the Paul Waverly meet and greet that had been set up at the end of the workday.

Cherie tried to convince her to go out for drinks and vent, but she declined. As close as she and Cherie had become since her arrival at WWDC, she'd never told her about Paul. That was a part of Layne's life that she tucked into a corner of her heart and soul.

She shut the door to her apartment, kicked off her shoes, dropped her tote on the floor next to her discarded shoes and dragged herself to the living room. Her cell phone chirped. She dug in the back pocket of her jeans and pulled out the phone. Tina's smiling face lit up the screen.

Layne's voice cracked when she tried to say hello.

"Layne? What's wrong?"

She heaved in a sob.

"Layne! What is it?"

"You won't freaking believe it," she managed, choking over the words.

"Believe what?"

"Paul. He's here in DC. *He* got the anchor job."

For a moment silence hung in the air until Tina sputtered a string of expletives. "I'm on my way." She didn't give Layne a chance to respond.

"So, Deanna somehow convinced Paul Waverly of all the men on the planet to come to DC to anchor the show that literally broke the two of you apart. Sh—" Tina spewed.

Layne sniffed back tears that had turned from hurt

and shock to anger. She finished off her second glass of wine, reached for one of the two bottles that Tina had brought with her and refilled her glass.

"I…I just don't even know what to think, to do."

"When is the last time you spoke to him?"

Layne sighed. "Been over two years," she said, the words like pinpricks to her heart.

"I take it Deanna has no clue about the two of you."

"I can't imagine how. If she does, she didn't hear it from me. No one knows, and since we never got a chance to announce our very brief engagement, no one back in Charlotte knew, either. I mean, thinking back to my meeting with her, I got the impression that she was bringing me on board but not entirely willingly." She shook her head. "That's about it. I don't even know." She sighed.

"Deanna has been known to be totally driven and has no problem stepping on and over folks to get what she wants. And the board loves her because of it. That's why it was so major that she agreed to bring you here." Tina sipped from her glass of wine. "Well, at some point you're going to have to talk to him. He knows you're here."

"Exactly! He knows I'm here. He knows how much I wanted this and yet—" She blew out a long breath of frustration. "You're right. We will have to talk at some point. We'll be working together." She nearly choked on the word *together.* "I'm going to have to get my head…and my heart together for the inevitable." She refilled her wineglass. "We need to order some food," she said and took a long sip, "before we move from just feeling good to not being able to feel!"

"Ha! You got that right. Pizza? Or something more substantial?"

"Two pies," Layne said, her gaze drifting off along with her thoughts. How could Paul have done this to her? Was it to punish her for leaving? Was that the man he'd become over the last three years—vindictive? She sighed. Sipped. Sighed.

Four

Paul walked into his rented apartment on Fifty-Ninth Street NW. He tugged his tie loose and unbuttoned his collar before crossing the high-glossed wood floors to the wet bar. WWDC didn't spare any expense or amenity. He poured a short tumbler of Hennessy, walked to the couch, reached for the remote and turned on the wall-mounted television. He scrolled through the channels and settled on a National Geographic special on Central Park in New York. He took a thoughtful sip as he watched the camera pan the milieu of Upper Westsiders. Most New Yorkers and ultimately much of the country could make a connection to the park because of the Central Park Five. Their notorious prosecution for a crime they didn't commit against a female jogger and their ultimate release and exoneration had dominated headlines. What many didn't know was that Central Park was once Seneca Village, owned and inhabited by a successful, thriving African American community in the mid-1800s, until the government deployed its power of eminent domain and took nearly 800 acres to build Central Park, the narrator explained.

He took another sip. Where did the people go? Seneca Village, Greenwood, Philadelphia? Those were the headline stories. But communities of color had been plagued and uprooted by either eminent domain or the other old-fashioned way—gentrification—for generations.

He changed the channel. Some things never changed, just the methods. A story for another day. He unbuttoned his white shirt and strolled into his bedroom. His living arrangements and location might have changed, but his feelings for Layne had not. He'd thought they had. He'd prayed for them to go away. For a while, burying himself in work and empty relationships had seemed to help. And then the offer had come from Deanna Mitchell.

A year earlier, he'd attended the annual convention of the National Association of Black Journalists in Chicago. He was one of the guest speakers touting the importance and relevance of local television and its ability to inform communities with the information and resources that could be used to make enlightened decisions.

After his talk, he was encircled by colleagues offering congratulations. Over the heads and shoulders, he'd spotted Deanna Mitchell, standing a bit off to the side, watching him over the rim of her wine flute. She smiled. But it wasn't a smile of acknowledgment or congratulations, it was something else.

One by one the congratulators had peeled off and Paul was face-to-face with Deanna. She was quite stunning, with her light olive complexion and startling, mint green eyes. She had the kind of features that made her origins hard to place, giving her an exotic quality. She moved catlike toward him.

"Mr. Waverly, wonderful presentation."

"Thank you." He gave a slight nod.

She extended her hand. "Deanna Mitchell, executive producer of *The DC Morning Show*."

Paul's jaw flexed. *DC Morning Show. Layne.*

"I was really impressed," Deanna was saying. "I've had an eye on your career for a while and I can tell you, going national will take you places you never imagined. You've outgrown local coverage."

Paul scoffed. "I'm almost complimented."

"You have to excuse my bluntness. I'm not always the best at being tactful."

His expression softened. "Whatever works."

Deanna laughed. "But I'm serious about what I said. You deserve more than a local spot. You have star power, Mr. Waverly. I know it when I see it." She reached in her clutch, pulled out an embossed business card and handed it to him. "In case you are ever in DC, please give me a call." She smiled and strutted away.

He briefly glanced at the card before tucking it into his inside jacket pocket. Layne was at WWDC and as much as he longed for her, it was not an offer he was prepared to accept. Besides, he had everything he could want exactly where he was. Everything except for Layne.

He put his meeting with Deanna Mitchell behind him, and dove body and soul into his work. It consumed him, keeping his longings at bay, except for the nights when the emptiness would overwhelm him and voluptuous, eager bodies didn't satisfy him.

Did she ever think of him, what they had? Did she ever regret leaving Charlotte? Had she found someone? Was she happy? When he was not immersed in work or buried in a willing body, those questions plagued him. Just when he'd finally reached a point where he could breathe without inhaling Layne's scent, Deanna Mitchell called, with an offer that literally stunned him. She truly made him an offer he would have been a fool to refuse.

Paul ran his hand across his face and close-cropped hair. Seeing Layne earlier had rocked him. A wave of emotions raced through him: shock, joy, anxiety and anger. It was the anger that seemed to linger. Seeing her again in the flesh and not in his dreams had reawakened the hurt and feeling of betrayal. And to see her get up and walk out—he huffed in annoyance. The move was a symbolic slap of dismissal.

He pushed out a breath and strode to the sauna-like bathroom to take a shower. Well, he was here now. He turned on the rain-head jet. Funny, the very spot that she so coveted was now his. The irony.

"Hey, girl, you good?" Cherie asked, meeting Layne in the hallway.

"It is what it is," she said and tried to smile.

They walked together down the corridor.

"Maybe he'll crash and burn," Cherie offered.

Layne snorted a laugh. Obviously, Cherie didn't know Paul Waverly. Crashing and burning was not in his MO. "Maybe," she said, knowing she didn't believe that for a moment. "I can't worry about Paul Waverly. I have my own job to focus on." She checked the time on her phone. "I have to prep for some interviews. They're breaking ground for another new shopping center that Montgomery Grant is backing."

"That brother is going to reshape inner city DC."

"Looks that way."

"Gotta run. I'll see you later." She picked up her pace and headed down the hall and into her office. She shut the door, pressed her back against it and closed her eyes.

Her heart was racing a mile a minute. She was sure that at any second Paul would walk around a corner or step out of a doorway and right into her path. What would she do then? What would they say to each other after all this time? Did they pretend they didn't know each other? That would be difficult, since Deanna knew they both hailed from WNCC.

She pushed away from the door and rounded her desk. She reached for the remote and pointed it at the television set mounted on the wall. *The DC Morning* show theme song and logo filled the screen and then there he was, making a brief cameo before his premiere.

The air hung in her chest. She tugged on her bottom lip with her teeth, watching Paul's marquee face fill the screen. His rugged voice filled her soul as he sat in conversation with Carl Bellows, who was filling in for Brett until Paul took over.

Transfixed, she saw Paul work the magic of his personality on any and everyone with the sound of his voice. There was no doubt that Paul Waverly was the consummate professional and would move into his new role as if it was made for him.

She sighed. Maybe it was. Maybe that anchor seat had never been hers to have. She blinked back the sting in her eyes and realized her hands were trembling. She balled her fingers into a fist. She'd given up so much to chase after a dream, only to find herself right back where she'd started.

How in the world was she going to be able to work every day? Following the show, there would be the team meeting that would go over the recording of the show to look for any hiccups to avoid next time, and set up the planning for the next show. She'd dodged a bullet for this show as it had been planned before Brett Conway was unceremoniously dismissed. But she couldn't avoid the debriefing session today, and prep for tomorrow's show, especially since she was responsible for doing two of the lead-in interviews for tomorrow's guests.

The DC Morning Show had another two hours before midday news came on. Layne had two hours to get her head on straight, look Paul Waverly in the eye, smile brilliantly and welcome him to the WWDC family. She groaned and buried her face in her hands.

The vibrating buzz of her cell phone forced her to open her eyes. Tina. She pressed the green icon.

"Hey, girl."

"Just checking on you. Want to make sure that you didn't slit your wrists or Paul's neck," she said with a snicker.

"Very funny. I'm good. I guess. I haven't seen him up close, only on screen, but that will change soon."

"How's that?"

Layne explained about the debriefing and prep.

"Oh, damn. Well, girl, you got this. He's just a man."

"Yeah."

"Um, I had another reason for calling. You know that as assistant editor here at the *Post*, I…uh… assign reporters to certain stories."

Layne's heart began to thud like a drumbeat that she could hear in her ears, like the dark music that plays when the unsuspecting victim senses something wrong in the dimly lit house. The audience knows. But she doesn't. Until it's too late.

"Whatever the hell it is, just say it!"

"We are assigning a reporter to cover Paul's first week at the station and do a close-up interview."

"You. Are. Freaking. Kidding Me!" Now her head was pounding.

Tina paused. "There's more."

"What the hell more could there be?" Her voice rose to the ceiling in a pitch high enough to shatter glass.

"I'm…the reporter."

Layne was pretty sure she'd just cussed out her best friend from here to the next millennium. She knew she'd stopped listening while Tina was trying to explain something about budget cuts and some other bs. She pressed her thumbs into her temples and slowly rotated them in the hopes of relieving the throbbing.

Truly, the world was conspiring against her. Must be that retrograde thing happening. Layne dragged in a breath and pushed to her feet. She tucked her laptop under her arm, stuck her cell phone in her jacket pocket and walked out of her office and down the hall toward the meeting room, reminding herself with every footstep—*you're a professional, you're a professional.*

Layne pushed open the heavy door, kept her expression blank and her eyes at half-mast as she inched her way around chairs and feet to find a seat as far in the back as possible.

Craig, the technical director, was up front making some adjustments to the recording equipment. He pointed the remote at the screen and *The DC Morning Show* logo appeared. He pressed pause and took a seat.

Cherie came rushing in, looked around, found Layne and headed in her direction, dragging an empty chair with her.

"Guess I didn't miss anything," she said in a conspiring whisper.

Layne crossed her ankles and propped her laptop on her thighs. "Not a thing."

Cherie dipped her head and leaned toward Layne. She cupped her hand around her mouth for added security. "I heard Deanna plans on showing up today and there's buzz going around that she's going to make a big announcement."

Layne's stomach rolled. She and big announcements were not doing so well together these days. "What more could she possibly tell us?" she said, each word dripping with sarcasm.

"Your guess is as good as mine."

Cherie settled back in her chair just as the door opened and Paul, accompanied by Deanna, walked in. They took seats up front. Craig stood. As technical director, he generally led these meetings with input from his team and the producer of the program.

While many might think this format was punitive, it was actually extremely helpful. Praise was always meted out and critiquing was done with care. Basically, it made everyone better at their jobs. It was very easy in this business to get tunnel vision and forget about all the other players on the game board. These briefings kept everyone grounded.

Once the program ended, Craig began by telling everyone that he believed it went extremely well, then pointed out some issues with lighting and the angle of one of the boom mics. He welcomed his new cameraperson, who happened to be a woman, much to everyone's delight.

Once Craig was done and questions and comments were addressed, Deanna moved to the front and faced the room.

"Here it comes," Cherie whispered from behind her hand.

Layne tapped her foot at a blinding rhythm.

"As usual, great job everyone. You all are the reason that *The DC Morning Show* has remained number two in our time slot." She extended her arm dramatically toward Paul. "And now that we have Paul Waverly anchoring, I have no doubt that we should be number one soon."

The room resounded with applause.

Deanna held her hand up. "I'll be monitoring our numbers, and with marketing and communications launching a full press on Paul's arrival, I have no doubt that the top spot will be ours and remain ours to stay." She beamed at the gathering, then turned her smile on Paul. She beckoned him to join her.

Paul walked to the front of the assembly, looking as handsome as always, in control yet humble all at the same time. It was a magical mix. There was something unique about Paul Waverly. He had what those in the business called the "it" factor. It was something that couldn't be explained in words, but only experienced. Paul had a way of combining a tilt of his head with a gentle lift of his mouth, and the slight lowering of his lids when he looked at you to make you think you were the most important person in the world. And his shine was not dimmed from behind a television screen. If anything, it was magnified. Every one of those attributes was on full display.

Paul smiled, slid his hands into his pockets. He swung a quick look at Deanna. "Thank you, Deanna. And thank all of you for an amazingly warm welcome. I'd promised myself early in my career that I'd never leave Charlotte. It was my home in more ways than one." He paused a beat. "But Deanna can be very persuasive," he said with a sardonic lift of his brow. The room tittered with laughter. "She's given me a heavy mantle to carry, but I'm sure that with the talent that's in this room, the weight will be light and the success will be ours because of all of you."

Layne rolled her eyes.

"And I have one more announcement to make," Deanna said. The team settled down. "Now that we are making some major adjustments to the face of the program, I think it's only fitting that Paul have one of our best to produce his show." She paused for effect. "Layne Davis."

"Oh sh—" Layne hissed from between her teeth.

Cherie clasped Layne's forearm. "Congrats, girl. That's major. A least he's not a stranger. Both of you from WNCC. And the fact that he is fine is a plus!"

Layne licked her lips and swallowed. Everyone turned toward her and clapped. She forced a smile. "Thank you, Deanna, everyone," she managed. "Very excited to be working with Mr. Waverly." She nearly choked on the faux sentiment. Her gaze jerked toward Paul and his was fixed on her. Her pulse thumped.

"Well." Deanna clapped her hands once. "That's it for today. Great job everyone. Layne," she called out over the rise of heads and shoulders. "Could you hang back for a minute?"

"Let's do lunch," Cherie said quietly. "I wanna know if he smells as good as I think he does," she giggled. "One o'clock at Mulberry's." She gathered her belongings and hurried to catch up with one of the technical assistants, better known as a TA.

Layne dragged out the process of slipping her laptop back in its case, arranging her chair back against the wall, checking the space for anything left behind, before straightening, dragging in a breath of resolve and moving through quicksand to the front of the room. Her heart began beating so hard and fast that it was hard to breathe. Her stomach did a slow roll.

"Layne Davis, Paul Waverly," Deanna said. "Paul, Layne is one of our best. As a matter of fact, she's done quite a bit of work in front of the camera as well." She smiled benevolently at Layne. "But of course you know that already. That's why I picked Layne."

"Good to see you again," Layne said. "Looking forward to working with you."

Paul's dark brown eyes flickered in a moment of uncertainty. He extended his hand and settled his gaze on her. "Nice to see you again, too. I've heard great things—from Deanna."

Layne swallowed. Her hand slipped into his. His fingers wrapped around hers and she may have gasped.

She cleared her throat. "Well, welcome to WWDC."

"I was hoping that we could sit down and talk about some ideas you may have and compare them with mine."

That raw silk voice was as mesmerizing as ever. If she didn't leave soon she would either faint or scream. "Sounds fine. Later today?"

"Say when?"

His smile made her sway on her feet.

"I think that's a great idea," Deanna suddenly cut in, angling her body so that she stood partially between Layne and Paul. "I'd like to sit in on that meeting. I have a few ideas of my own that I'd like to share with you, Paul. And we can discuss your upcoming interview with the *Post*." She turned to Layne. "I believe the reporter is an acquaintance of yours, Tina Gerard," she said, her expression and tone making clear that she knew Tina had a hand in getting Layne her interview and ultimately her job.

Layne cleared her throat and lifted her chin. "Yes. She is."

"I'm open any time after three," Paul said, cutting in.

"Let's do four, in my office," Deanna said. She flashed a tight smile at Layne.

Layne drew in a breath. "Perfect," she said, lifting her brows and widening her eyes in fake delight. "I'll see you both then." She flashed a smile. "I'm sorry. I've got to run. The show must go on." She spun away and out the door on shaky legs and a thudding heart.

Paul walked out with Deanna until they parted ways in front of his office.

"See you at four," Deanna said before whisking away.

Paul opened the door and stepped into his corner office. He shut the door behind him, tugged his tie loose and shrugged out of his jacket. He hung the jacket on the coatrack and crossed the tan carpeted floor to the well-stocked bar. It was barely past one but he needed a drink.

He poured a short shot of Hennessy and tossed it back in one gulp. He was rattled. There was no other word for it. Seeing Layne again. That close. Inhaling her. Remembering. But she'd looked at him with the same emptiness in her eyes that she'd left in his heart when she'd moved from Charlotte.

So it was a game they would play. The game of not knowing each other beyond a casual acquaintance. The game of indifference. The game of keeping it professional.

He strode to the window. The circular outline of the US Capitol Building sprawled below him. He slung his hands into his pockets and drew in a long, slow breath. His jaw clenched reflexively. He shot his cuffs and checked the platinum Rolex—ironically a gift from Layne on his thirty-fifth birthday. Three hours. Three hours and they would be face-to-face. Nowhere to run. Nowhere to hide. Let the games begin.

"Wow. This whole thing just gets weirder by the minute," Tina was saying into the phone. "You have been assigned to be his producer? I'll be damned. Hey, maybe it's a sign."

As annoyed as she'd been with her bestie earlier, she knew Tina wouldn't do anything to intentionally hurt her. She was doing her job and she was damned good at it. Besides, who was she going to rant and rave and freak out to about Paul if not Tina?

"A sign of what? The apocalypse?"

Tina sputtered a laugh. "Damn, girl, it's not that bad. Really. I mean, think about it. It's been three years. Both of you have had time to come to terms with your life. You both made some hard choices."

Layne sighed. "That's all rational and whatnot. But it doesn't account for—" her voice hitched "—how I feel."

"How do you feel?" Tina asked softly.

Layne pressed the cell phone to her cheek. "I feel… everything. Sad. Confused. Angry. Gut-punched."

"But do you still love him, Layne?"

"I don't want to," she said on a breath.

As much as Layne thought she wasn't up for Cherie's chatter, lunch with her coworker actually loosened the knots in her stomach. Cherie had a no-filter personality, and combined with their favorite comfort food—burgers and fries—and the conversations ebbing and flowing around them, Layne felt much steadier on her feet when she walked through the doors of Deanna Mitchell's office. At least until Paul turned from his seat and unmoored her with a single look when she entered.

For an instant, she faltered, but she quickly recovered.

"Layne, please join us," Deanna said magnanimously. She waved her over to the small conference table. "Would you like anything? Coffee, water?" She extended her hand to the setup on the center of the table.

"No, thank you. I'm fine." She sat and put her laptop on the smooth wood surface of the table. She flipped the lid open and pressed the power button. Paul was barely two feet away. She could feel the heat of his body. It wafted with that familiar—more natural than high-end, store-bought—scent that seeped into her pores, the way it always had. Her insides quaked.

"So," Deanna began, "I hope you are as excited as I am about this pairing," she said to Layne.

"Absolutely. This is a fantastic opportunity."

"I think so, too," Paul added. "Deanna has been singing your praises and you had a solid reputation back at WNCC—from what I can recall."

Layne swallowed. Her gaze flicked in his direction and then away. "You said you had some ideas, Deanna?"

"Yes." She tilted her head toward Paul. "A great deal is riding on you. I had to pull too many strings to name in order to get you here. But I know it will be worth it, and to ensure that it is, at least for the first month, I want to review and approve everything that goes on the air."

Layne's brow lifted. As executive producer, of course Deanna had that option, but she rarely chose it. She oversaw the producers, staff and budget, and she also was ED for *Nightwatch*, the after-eleven-o'-clock news show—enough to keep her hands full. For her to get into the weeds of *The DC Morning Show* meant that there really was a lot on the line and it was more than ratings.

Paul folded his arms across his chest but didn't comment.

"You've been an assistant producer, but stepping up to producer is going to take even more work. Every element of the program is up to you. Of course, you will work hand in hand with Paul and get his approval along the way."

"Of course." Layne licked her lips. "I want to put together my own team."

Deanna nodded in agreement. "You'll run the names by me."

Layne blinked. On one hand Deanna claimed to bestow her with so much power, and with the other hand kept a grip on it.

"Sure."

"Prepare a list of names for your team. Get them to me by tomorrow morning. I'd like them all approved and assembled in the Writers' Room by lunch." She turned to Paul. "Any show ideas that you have, contacts for interview guests, topics you want to go after, get them to Layne and she will make it happen. In the meantime, we'll finish out Brett's schedule."

The corner of Paul's lush mouth lifted into a half grin. "Not a problem." He slid a look in Layne's direction.

"That's all I have," Deanna said, signaling the end of the meeting. "Keep me in the loop." She placed her palms flat on the table. "Oh, and you might want to keep tabs on the progress with the interview—with your friend."

Layne didn't miss the dig. She rose. "I'd better get working on that list." She gave Paul a short nod and walked out.

Her pulse roared in her ears. She had to keep blinking to keep the space in front of her in focus. What in the entire hell had happened back there? She stabbed the elevator button and paced until the doors slid open. She stepped forward and, when she turned, caught a glimpse of Paul coming toward her. She stepped fully inside and frantically pressed the button for the main floor. An instant before the doors slid shut, Paul's face appeared and then it was gone. The elevator began its descent.

* * *

Layne spent the rest of her afternoon putting together her list of who she wanted on her team. Although she'd put programs together in the past, it had always been in a secondary role. This time it was all on her. If the show flopped, it would be on her, and if she had any intention of moving to that anchor chair, screwing up was not an option. Not to mention that there was only one anchor seat. Her other obstacle was that Paul was sitting in it.

Five

Paul snorted a laugh as the elevator door slid shut. He should take it as a metaphor for his relationship with Layne—closed. He boarded the next elevator to the main floor of the studio. He walked down the hallway, passed partially open office doors and bustling technicians and staff. He nodded, smiled and murmured thanks to well-wishers as he strode toward his corner office. His step slowed when he got in front of Layne's door. It was closed, but he could hear murmurs of a one-sided conversation. He hesitated, raised his hand to knock but changed his mind. He continued on to his office.

Paul discarded his jacket on the couch and loosened his tie. One full day under his belt. It was easier than he'd imagined. He'd spent his career in front of a camera, reading notes and teleprompters and convincing the viewing audience that what he said could be trusted. What was hard was seeing Layne again. Seeing her up close, hearing her voice, inhaling her familiar scent had been more difficult than he'd imagined.

He kicked off his shoes and took them to the bedroom, sliding them onto the shoe rack. He sat down on the edge of the bed, then flopped back, tucked his hands behind his head and stared up at the ceiling. The hardest part wasn't seeing Layne, it was experiencing her impervious reaction to him. He was sure part of it was akin to how they had to be around each other in North Carolina. They'd grown used to pretending to be no more than colleagues. But it was more than that. There was now an icy wall that she'd erected.

He'd taken this job against all of his vows to himself because it would put him back in Layne's path, and give them both a chance to start over or at least pick up where they'd left off. Compounded with the fact that the deal for him to host his own talk show remained in limbo and added to the last push he needed to leave WNCC.

His cell phone vibrated in his pocket. He dug the phone out and smiled at the name illuminated on the face.

"Hey, man," Paul sat up and greeted his brother, Eric.

"Hey. Congrats. Me and Tricia just watched your debut on the DVR. Not bad."

Paul chuckled. "Gee, thanks, bro."

"So, how was the first day? Did you see Layne?"

"First day was better than I expected. The people are really cool, made me feel like part of the team."

"And Layne…?" Eric hedged.

Paul exhaled. "I saw her."

"And?"

"Hard. Awkward."

After some more prodding, Paul explained everything that happened.

"So you didn't actually talk to each other."

"No. I started to stop by her office but changed my mind."

"Hmm, well, she could simply be going along with the same program y'all set up back in NC. Keeping a low profile."

"Yeah. I figure the same thing."

"At some point you're gonna have to have a conversation, especially if she is producing your shows."

"Hmm, there's that." He got to his feet and walked to the windows that looked out over the nation's capital and wondered if leaving everything behind in North Carolina and coming to DC had been a monumental mistake.

Layne parked her car in the underground garage of Essex House, using Tina's guest parking spot. She grabbed her laptop bag and small overnight tote and walked to the elevator, taking it to the eighth floor.

She exited the elevator and wound her way around the circular layout to Suite 8C. She pressed the buzzer and, moments later, Tina flung open the door and exuberantly greeted her friend.

"Let the shenanigans begin," she said kissing Layne's cheek. She draped an arm around Layne's shoulder and ushered her inside.

Tina's two-bedroom was airy and spacious and furnished with an Afrocentric flair, from the bold colored accessories on the deep navy blue seating of the six-foot sectional, chaise and club chair, to the art-work and wooden figurines that made the entire space a showroom—but cozy at the same time.

"Make yourself comfortable, sis. I thought we could have dinner downstairs. Rumor has it that Chef Alonzo Grant is visiting and will be overseeing the menu," she said with a gleam in her eyes.

"Sounds great." Layne stepped out of her shoes and shrugged out of her light jacket before following Tina into the living area.

"Wine?"

"Sure."

Tina poured them each a flute and joined Layne on the couch. "Really glad you came. Things kinda went left between us and I wanted to make sure we were good, ya know."

Layne nodded. "I know. I was totally overreacting. This whole Paul thing has me off-center."

"I get it. So we'll do dinner, talk and plan," Tina said with a wink.

Layne lifted her glass. "To plans."

"How do you see this working relationship turning out?" Tina asked as she cut into her striped bass.

"I'm a professional and he's a professional." Layne

took a spoonful of risotto. "Hmm, this is delicious," she murmured.

"Told ya." Tina wagged her fork. "I'm going to be honest with you." She put down her fork and wiped her mouth with the cloth napkin. "You made a decision three years ago to follow your dream. Your dream resulted in a breakup with the man you were in love with. But three years later you still haven't snatched that star that you ran after. Not quite. And here comes the man that you put everything on the line for and he takes that seat you wanted for yourself. Totally f'd up. But that is your reality. And I'm not sure what you're most upset about—that for all you gave up, it's still out of reach or that Paul got what you wanted."

Layne sighed heavily and slowly shook her head. "Both. Everything and then some," she said, her voice arching. "When I left Charlotte for this job I believed in my bones that it would only be a matter of time until I got the seat. All I had to do was prove myself by producing quality content. Chasing the right stories to air, knowing the ropes." She blinked rapidly. "But none of that mattered because they didn't *see* me—really see me." She tugged on her bottom lip with her teeth for a moment. "But they will. I'm gonna be the best damned producer *The DC Morning Show* has ever had. I'm going to produce an Emmy-winning show with me at the anchor desk. And Paul Waverly is going to wish he'd stayed in Charlotte, North Carolina." She raised her glass and brought it to her lips. "That's the plan," she said and took a sip.

Tina lifted her glass. "Cheers to that."

* * *

Spending the evening with her best friend was as regenerating as their times together usually were. They talked, they laughed, debated and talked some more. They picked through the landmine of Tina doing an interview with Paul, with her promising to remain totally objective and that she would not allow their friendship to shape the story.

"I wouldn't expect anything less. You have your journalistic integrity to uphold. Paul knows that you and I are friends. Deanna knows that we're friends."

"All very incestuous," Tina teased.

"Ha! But seriously, we're all here to do our best." She covered Tina's hand with her own, as they wrapped up their evening with a nightcap on Tina's couch.

So, when Layne walked into the station the following morning, there was a new confidence in her step, a lift to her chin. She'd sent her recommendations for her team, via email, to Deanna, before she'd gone to bed, and found Deanna's approval in her morning email.

Buoyed with confidence, she booked one of the small conference rooms to host a debriefing and introduce the team members to each other. Today was the last day of Brett's program schedule. Beginning Monday, the show would be handed off to her and her new team.

While the technical staff and camera crew all knew each other, many had not worked together as a unit before. The balance of the day would include confirming responsibilities, partnerships and a pitch session with the writers. And, of course, sitting across the table from Paul.

"Good morning, folks," Layne greeted as she walked into the control room. The morning news had just ended and the station was in commercial break before handing the programming over to their affiliate stations.

"As you all know, I've gotten the dream assignment to produce *The DC Morning Show with Paul Waverly.*" There was a smattering of applause, mixed with faux grunts and groans of protest. Layne grinned. "Anyway, we have to hit the ground running. You all will be happy to know that I have requested each of you to be on my team." This time the approval was real. "I've reserved the second-floor conference room—and lunch," she added with a grin. "I'll be expecting everyone at one sharp. Bring your energy, ideas and appetite. Cool?" She flashed a smile, walked out and headed to her office. As she turned the corner she ran, literally, into Paul.

"Oh." She clutched her iPad to her chest. "Paul."

He stretched out a steadying hand. His fingers lightly clasped her upper arm. "Layne."

Her breath hitched. "Sorry. Wasn't paying attention." She started to move around him.

"It *is* good to see you," he said quietly.

Her stomach quivered. She swallowed and forced a tight smile. "I'll see you at the m-meeting…one o'clock," she stammered before hurrying off.

Once behind her closed office door, she allowed her emotions to escape in a slow but steady stream of tears that felt endless, as if by expelling this dam of pain she could make it dry up until nothing but a dust bowl remained.

She made her way to the small two-seat sofa and curled into the corner of it, drawing her knees to her chest. She rested her head on the arm and let the tears flow until, after what seemed like forever, they finally slowed to a drizzle, then a sprinkle, and then a drip, like the last hurrah of a sudden thunderstorm in summer.

She blinked. Her eyes felt heavy and she knew she must look a hot mess. She unfurled her body and her joints ached. Slowly, she got to her feet and rotated her neck and shoulders, then went to her desk, opened the bottom drawer and took out her purse. She rummaged around for a mirror and gasped at the sight of her puffy face. She looked like she'd spent the night out drinking. The key now was getting to the ladies' room and avoiding curious looks, so she could repair the damage done by the floodgates.

She grabbed her bag and feeling like a spy crossing enemy lines, she hurried—head lowered and eyes fixed on her iPad—down the hall to the ladies' room. She tapped the code in the door lock panel and pushed the door open. There was a flush in the distance.

Layne went to the sink and turned on the cold water, quickly splashing water on her face, just as one of the interns exited the stall. She gave Layne a brief glance, washed her hands and walked out.

Layne snatched some paper towels from the dispenser and dried her face. She peered closer at her reflection. Fortunately, she didn't wear much makeup, if any at all except for special occasions. So the repairs were minimal. Her mascara had left dark smudges under her eyes. *So much for non-streaking mascara.* She cleaned up her eyes with the baby wipes she always kept in her bag and reapplied her mascara. She checked for any remnants of salty streaks on her face, then dabbed some clear lip gloss on her mouth and a light moisturizer to her face. One more close look, then she took a step back.

The slight wrinkles of her bright white blouse were hidden beneath a navy jacket over fitted dark jeans. She looked every bit the producer that she was, ready to meet her team—and face Paul.

The second-floor conference room was one of the smaller of the four in the building and could still easily accommodate twenty to twenty-five. The ten-foot table allowed for plenty of work space and the table was equipped with embedded outlets for computers, tables and smartphones. The front of the room had a massive screen that took up one wall, and a small podium for speakers to make presentations.

By the time Layne arrived, the vendor delivering lunch had just finished setting out the trays of sandwiches, salads and refreshments on a long table against the wall. Urns of coffee, tea and lemonade sat at one end.

"Thank you so much," Layne said to the delivery team. "Looks great."

"There are extra plates and utensils under the skirt of the table, in case," the young woman offered.

"Great. Thank you."

The team began filing in and by ten minutes after one everyone was seated with a plate of food in front of them.

"Will Mr. Waverly be joining us?" one of the techs asked.

Layne cleared her throat. "He—"

"Yes, I am," Paul cut in as he walked into the room. "I apologize for being late. Was in another meeting." He gave a short nod to Layne and smiled around the room.

"Um, grab a plate. Your seat is right there," she said, pointing to an empty space near the front. "We were just about to get started, so you haven't missed anything," Layne said, the most words she'd uttered to him since his arrival.

Layne flipped on the big screen that projected the information from her iPad and launched into her presentation, beginning with assignments, partnerships and scheduling. She gave everyone a chance to weigh in and got agreements all around before moving to the on-air assignments that went to Kevin Parker, who had a knack for targeted coverage of major events. He would handle breaking news. She and Kevin had worked together before and she was happy to give him a solo shot in the limelight. Della Bryant was an up-and-coming journalist who was as smart as she was camera-ready. Her specialty was political science with a twist of economics. There was plenty for her to cover in this town. Layne partnered her with Carmen Fuentes, who had the experience and the graciousness to bring a newcomer along. International Affairs went to Simon Fields. No one at WWDC was as good as Simon at what he brought to the table. Layne gave him his choice of a partner to back him up and he surprised everyone by selecting Adrienne Allen, who'd been with the company for a bit more than a year. Adrienne had shown talent by bringing hard-to-reach stories to the surface, but had yet to really spread her wings.

The meeting moved smoothly with barely a hiccup. Layne was ecstatic with how things were working out. Her newly minted team seemed genuinely pleased with their assignments and most of all with the opportunity to be heard.

Once that part of the heavy lifting was completed, the on-air members were set up with their roving crew. The crew members, once assigned, bade their goodbyes.

Now the next phase began, the pitch session and planning out Paul's programming for the upcoming week. Layne was relieved that she didn't have to deal with Paul directly but rather through the team, who pitched and tossed ideas until they had a go-ahead from Paul, cosigned by Layne. "If that's what the anchor wants, that's what the anchor gets," she said more than a half dozen times.

More than four hours later, exhausted but satisfied, she was ready to wrap up, with every piece of *The DC Morning Show with Paul Waverly* in place.

The marketing department had already changed

the set. Now he had his own theme music and a tagline. *The DC Morning Show* was the only network program in that time slot that did not have a co-anchor. It made it unique but it also put a great burden on the host to carry the program from start to finish for nearly two hours.

"Well, I think that covers everything," Layne said, the fatigue beginning to overtake the earlier rush of adrenaline. "I am very pleased with how things shaped up. I'll need each of you to have some drafts ready and any footage or cues that will be needed in the control room."

There were nods all around.

"We'll have our daily meetings directly after the show ends so we stay on track."

"Agreed."

"I'll be handling all the booking of guests, and approving or disapproving of costs. You need to have me as a friend," Cherie added with a wink.

"Unless there are any other concerns or questions..." Layne glanced around the table. "Great. Thanks, everyone." She gathered up her belongings as bodies began filing out.

When she looked up, Paul was still seated. Her heart thumped. She started for the door. Paul rose in a blur.

"Wait."

She glanced back at him from over her shoulder. "I'm really busy."

"Layne, please. We need to talk."

She turned fully around. "Do we, Paul? Really? About what? About how you wouldn't support me in my dream to come here to get *that* spot!" Her voice rose. "The spot that you swept in and took! Of all the jobs on the damned planet." She began to pace, her voice and thoughts racing. "Your personal mantra was that you'd never leave Charlotte. Never. Not even for me, Paul." Her eyes burned. She blinked back tears. "Yet— Here. You. Are," she spewed. "When it all became about you," she said, her tone dripping with disgust. "So, no, there's nothing to talk about, Paul, unless it's about the show." Her smile was a slash of her mouth. "I'll do my job and you do yours." She brushed by him and out, her heart pounding so hard and she felt slightly dizzy.

By the time she reached her office and was able to sit down, her entire body was shaking, and she had her second crying jag of the day.

Paul walked to his office, collected his things and headed to the parking garage. Layne's vehemence shook him. The look in her eyes, the deep hurt and fury, cut to his core. His decision to come to DC and take this job had been two-fold, but was it primarily selfish and self-serving as Layne accused? Had he really allowed the bright lights of national fame to blind him to what his coming here would do to her—even though his real reason was that he wanted to be near her, wanted her back and maybe even to prove to himself that he could make it on the national stage?

The sound of his shoes cracking across the concrete floor of the garage echoed in the emptiness of his soul. What had he done?

"Hey, there."

Paul stopped, turned. Deanna was walking toward him. "Hi." He adjusted the strap of his leather satchel on his shoulder.

"So, how did the meeting go today? Get everything you need?"

She stood inches in front of him. The green of her eyes sparkled in this light, he noticed. "Went well. Layne has put together an impressive team."

She angled her head to the side, studied him. "Glad to hear that." Her brow tightened. "Everything okay?"

"Yes. Absolutely."

"If you don't have immediate plans, how about a wind-down drink? Great place right around the corner."

"Wow. Thanks for the invite. I'm kinda beat, have a lot of notes to go over. Rain check?"

"Of course." She drew in a breath and released her reply. "Well, get some rest. We need you bright and ready on Monday."

"Sure thing. Good night." He offered a tight smile, turned and walked down the next aisle to his reserved parking spot. Layne had made herself perfectly clear: They had nothing to discuss—at least nothing that she wanted to hear from him. He put the car in gear and eased around the lanes toward the exit. If that was how she wanted things to be between them, then maybe now was the time to do what she wanted.

Layne was literally biting her manicured nails as the music rose and the logo for *The DC Morning*

Show with Paul Waverly splashed across the screen. Her heart thumped as she listened to the technical director cue camera one. And there he was. She held her breath, not because she was concerned that Paul would fumble the touchdown, but that something else would go wrong and she would be the only one responsible. This was, after all, her show. Paul Waverly's name might be the marquee attraction, but it was her ass on the line if anything went left.

Cherie came to stand behind her. She squeezed Layne's shoulder. "Damn, he's good," she said, kind of in awe, as Paul smoothly moved from one headline to the next, knowing just when to turn his gaze, lower his voice, raise a brow or stare directly into the camera.

"Yeah. He is," she said on a breath.

The segment broke for a weather update.

Layne turned away from the multiple screens in the control room deck and went to the desk that contained the playbook. She flipped the cover open and ran over the storyboard: international news, economics, two location reports, then back to Paul for updates from Capitol Hill. The news would be fed to him in his earpiece and projected on the teleprompter. Then, another weather break and back to Paul for his interview with Senator Hamilton and his run for reelection.

The first hour was in the can and the second hour almost done. Layne paced, watched the monitors and paced some more, studying every move, every signal, every segue. And then it was over. Paul gave his trademark goodbye, held the audience in his gaze for that one extra moment, and then the screen went to commercial. A whoop of happiness and a bevy of praise was showered on Layne for her first time up producing a major program. Her spirits lifted, but she took the accolades in stride. One great show did not an Emmy-winning program make.

Stagehands darted on set to remove microphones, notes and electrical cords in preparation for *News at Noon*, followed by Tess Hampton's cooking show.

The studio door swung open and Paul walked in. The team erupted in applause and rounds of congratulations.

Paul held up his hand. "I came in here—" his gaze swept the room "—to thank all of you for doing an incredible job. You made my work a breeze."

He flashed that million-dollar smile and Layne's stomach tumbled. His eyes found her in the semi-darkness. He gave her a short nod.

"Thank you, everyone. Back at it tomorrow." He gave a thumbs-up and walked out.

Layne finally breathed once the door closed behind Paul. "Thanks, everyone. Debriefing at one," she reminded them and headed out. Cherie was on her heels.

"Big congratulations, Layne," Cherie was saying as they walked down the corridor. "Everything moved like clockwork."

"Definitely a team effort," Layne said.

"Good leadership. Hey," she said, when they stopped in front of Layne's office, "I know you were hoping for the anchor spot, but maybe this is a blessing in disguise." Layne frowned in confusion. "You pull off a solid season with this show, take it to number one and you can write your own ticket—executive producer, maybe even pitch your own show." Her brows lifted for emphasis.

"Hmm." She'd been so focused on being furious with Paul and just getting the first show successfully off the ground that she hadn't really thought that far ahead or the possibilities. "One day at a time," she finally said while opening her door.

"Put it out in the atmosphere," Cherie said. "Speak it into existence." She patted Layne's arm. "See you at the debrief." She continued down the hallway.

Layne walked into her office and shut the door behind her. She dropped her iPad on her desk and felt the tight cords that were holding her body together slowly begin to unwind. She drew in a long breath and let her eyes close in a moment of pure relief. Maybe there was some validity to what Cherie said. Maybe it was finally time to reimagine her future in broadcasting. However, the pill of Paul Waverly being here at WWDC was still hard to swallow.

The first weeks of *The DC Morning Show* went smooth as butter. The team worked seamlessly together and Paul was being the charismatic star that he was reputed to be. Everyone *loved* him. Inwardly, Layne groaned as she listened to the accolades tossed around with Paul's name attached. But she had to admit that things were going better than she'd anticipated. During the briefing sessions, Paul was agreeable to the lineups and the topics and Layne's vision for each show. She was slowly beginning to accept his presence and secretly looked forward to seeing him, hearing his voice—remembering. To add to her sense of contentment, Tina had found another reporter to interview Paul and assured her it wouldn't take more than two days the following week to finish it. The interview was over and the article slated to run at the end of the month.

And then, three weeks in, all that glittered turned to something on the bottom of a shoe. Paul began to question Layne's decisions and then challenging her choices for guests, as well as what she was assigning the team to cover. At first she shrugged it off as Paul finally getting comfortable in his role and wanting to get his feet wet with more input. But his displeasure only seemed to grow as he found something to critique about pretty much everything Layne suggested. It got bad enough that halfway through Paul's first month, Deanna called Layne to her office.

"Layne, come in and have a seat."

Layne crossed the threshold and her stomach rolled when she spotted Paul sitting at the end of the small conference table intent on his smartphone. He barely looked up when she entered.

Deanna got up from behind her desk and walked over to the table with a folder in hand. "I won't waste time with small talk. Paul is unhappy with how you have been handling things with the program."

Layne slowly sat down. She flashed Paul a look but he acted as if she wasn't there.

Deanna's green eyes were dark, her normally olive complexion was flushed, and her red-polished lips drawn into a tight line. She flipped open the folder. "Over the past week, Mr. Waverly has brought to my attention his…concern with some of the choices you have made with the program. For example, moving the segments around just as he was getting accustomed to the order, and setting up interviews with guests who aren't newsworthy. Besides, the debriefing sessions are not as productive as they need to be or at least as they had been when he first arrived."

Layne swallowed. "When I was given the assignment to produce this program I was also given the responsibility to run it successfully—and I have. Ratings are up and growing. We were number one in our time slot last week, the second week in a row." Her head swiveled toward Paul, her temper boiling. "Mr. Waverly may not be accustomed to the way I do things, but my job is to run a successful show and team—not hand-hold a—"

"I'd watch myself if I were you, Ms. Davis," Deanna cut in. "It might be your show to run, but without the star, you would be back on the street chasing stories and in the office booking guests. Whether you want to or not, you will get Mr. Waverly's approval *and* mine going forward, until this miscommunication is back on track. Does that work for you, Paul?"

He tilted his head slightly to the side, a half smile curving his mouth. "Works fine. Thanks, Deanna."

Layne was so hurt and humiliated she couldn't speak. She gripped the edge of the table and rose to her feet. "Anything else?" Her knees felt wobbly.

"Nothing else for now. Thank you for coming in, Layne. I'm sure that working together, we can get over this minor bump in the road."

Layne blinked to push back the clouds that obscured her vision, turned and walked out.

Paul didn't need to make any more complaints. He'd successfully shaken her confidence to a point where she questioned her own decisions and constantly second-guessed herself. And it was becoming obvious to her team as well.

"Layne," Cherie said, sidling up to her friend after the weekly planning meeting. "What the heck is going on with you?" she asked in a harsh whisper.

Layne just lowered her head and slowly shook it. "Tired."

"Don't play with me. Tired never bothered you before. It's Paul. He has you off your game. What is going on? Did you rub him the wrong way or something?"

"Just has the 'I am the star' syndrome," Layne murmured.

"Well, whatever it is, it's taking the shine off *your* star. And I don't like it. I don't like what it's doing to you."

"I'll be fine." She offered a tight smile. "I'm going

to take the weekend off and just relax for a change. Programming is mapped out for the next two weeks barring something unforeseen. So I'm going to put this place behind me for this long weekend."

"Good. You deserve it. Any special plans?"

"Not really. Playing it by ear."

"My sister is having her annual cookout. Nothing can compare to a backyard full of family, tipsy on beer and ribs, with access to fireworks. What could possibly go wrong?" Cherie said laughing.

Layne chuckled. "Let's hope your family doesn't make the eleven o'clock news."

"Girl, you and me both. Take care. Enjoy. See you next week. You have my number if you want to come and hang out."

"Thanks."

They parted ways and Layne went to her office to check last-minute emails and pack up. There was an email from Deanna, wanting to meet on Tuesday, after the holiday, to get an update on the programming.

Layne stared at the words and the anger that she'd struggled for weeks to suppress rose from the soles of her feet, heating her blood until her temples throbbed and her breath hitched in short spurts. Tears of fury stung her eyes, but she was tired of crying, tired of being undermined. She wanted her job but not like this. It wasn't worth it. *He* wasn't worth it. Enough!

She snatched up her bag and stormed toward the

door, tugged it open and came face-to-face with Paul, with his fist frozen inches before knocking.

Layne's mouth opened in surprise.

"Please, I need to talk to you," Paul whispered.

Six

Layne was stunned speechless. She'd been on her way to have it out with Paul and maybe lose her job in the process, and here he was—wanting to talk!

"Please," he asked again.

"You've done everything short of asking Deanna to fire me. You question every decision I make, undermine me at every turn in front of my team." Her chest heaved.

She was so furious she didn't even realize that Paul had stepped in and shut the door behind him.

Her eyes blazed.

"Why, damn it? Tell me why! You came all this way to ruin everything I've done for myself. Why?" Her voice cracked.

He slowly shook his head. "It… It's not like that. I want to explain. I'll explain everything over dinner."

"Are you out of your mind?"

"No. Listen." He tried to reach for her and she jerked back. He held up his hands in surrender. "You have every right and reason to feel the way you do about me…about everything. I was wrong. I was angry and I was selfish."

Layne heaved a breath and folded her arms tightly across her chest. She rested her weight on her right hip and glowered at him.

"I want to make it up to you. All of it, and I will if you let me."

"It's too late, Paul."

He took a step toward her. "I don't think it is." His gaze trailed over her face. "I know it isn't. If you'll just hear me out. Please…"

She felt the rod in her back soften.

"After you hear what I have to say, then whatever you say or do—" he released a breath "—I'll never bother you again. And I'll do everything I can to make your job easier. Starting with not being a pain in the ass."

Layne snickered against her will.

"Just an hour. We don't even have to do dinner if you don't want. Drinks? Talk?"

Damn it, when he looked at her like that. Layne tipped her head to the side and licked her lips. "You said dinner." She rolled her eyes. "Well… Let's go. Julian's is great and it's walking distance," she said, brushing by him.

Paul stood in dutiful silence next to Layne on the way down on the elevator. He was moderately thankful that they were the only riders. The two-block walk to the restaurant was a different story. It might be July but the temperature between the two of them was below freezing. She barely acknowledged his existence as they wound their way around the after-fivers looking for a place to unwind at the end of the workday and the entrée to a long weekend.

They stopped in front of Julian's. Paul opened the door. Layne rolled her eyes again and walked inside.

They walked in silence to the hostess's podium.

"Seating or bar?" the hostess asked with a practiced smile.

"Seating for dinner," Layne said.

"There is about a half-hour wait. I can take your name if you want to sit at the bar. You'll be called when your table is ready."

"That sounds fine," Layne said. "Davis."

The hostess made a note. "You'll be called."

"Thank you." Layne walked off to the bar, leaving Paul in her wake.

She found the last empty seat and slid onto the stool. Paul stood next to her.

"Still drinking margaritas?" he asked.

She angled her head toward him in slow motion. She wouldn't give him the satisfaction of being right. "No. Frozen apple martini."

Paul flicked a brow, then signaled for the bartender. "Frozen apple martini and Hennessy on the rocks, please."

Layne stared ahead, not daring to look at him and risk giving in. Being this close to him, with his body nearly pressing against her, it took all her willpower not to lean into him, the way she once had.

The bartender put their drinks in front of them.

Layne lifted her glass toward her lips. “So…you got me here. I’m listening. What do you have to say?”

“I still love you, Layne,” he murmured.

She sputtered the sweet liquid and flashed him a look of disbelief. “Wh-what?”

“I never stopped loving you.” He moved closer so that there was nothing between them but air. “I was a fool and too full of my ego to see it.” He lowered his head a moment, then looked into her astonished face. “I never intended to take the job but then I realized that coming here, I could be with you again, try to make it work. If you were willing to step out on faith, why couldn’t I?”

“It’s been three years,” Layne said. “Not a word from you.”

He drew in a breath. “I know. I was stubborn and hurt. But being without you ate away at me every day. When Deanna approached me with the offer, I turned her down. Then she told me about six months ago that there were ‘problems’ with Brett and that if he was let go, she wanted me for the spot.”

Layne slowly shook her head. “She also knew that I’d been working toward it.”

“That I didn’t know. I thought that if she offered it, you weren’t interested anymore. And from everything I’ve seen since I’ve been here, you are one helluva producer.”

She scoffed. "You'd never know it by your behavior."

"Stupid. For some reason that makes no sense I thought if I ticked you off enough it would force you to talk to me. Even if it meant lashing out." He took a chance and reached out to stroke her cheek with the tip of his finger. Her lids fluttered. "I love you. I want the chance to make everything up to you. Everything, whatever it takes. But what ultimately made me take the offer was that not having you in my life made me realize I was only living halfway, going through the motions."

"Davis!" a waitress called out.

Paul glanced over his shoulder. "Table is ready." He helped her to her feet, thankful that she didn't smack his hand away.

They reviewed the menu in silence. Layne wasn't sure if she could eat a thing when her salmon salad arrived. Her mind was spinning, trying to make sense of what Paul confessed. He still loved her.

When she'd left Charlotte three years ago, her heart was broken in ways she could never put into words. She'd buried herself in her work to block out the loneliness and wondered every day if she'd made the right decision. She'd been on her way up back in Charlotte, but she was so fixed on this damned show that she'd given it up. And for what? She still didn't have what she thought she'd wanted, when what she'd really only wanted was being with Paul—doing this thing they loved—together.

"So…how did they take it at the station when you told them you were leaving?" Layne quietly asked.

Paul smothered a laugh and wiped his mouth with the napkin. "Let's just say it was an uproar." He went on to tell her about the emergency meetings, the promises, the added perks, the apologies for his talk show not materializing. They'd even gone so far as to say that they'd hold his spot for six months no questions asked, if he decided to come back.

"What?" Layne squeaked, wide-eyed.

"Yep."

"So does Deanna know about this six-month deal?"

He nodded.

"Wow, you really are a rock star."

He leaned across the table and took her hand. "I figured if I couldn't win you back in six months…"

"I don't know what to say," she said slowly.

"Say you'll think about it. That's all I ask."

She reached for her drink and took a sip and then another. "I'll…think about it."

His smile lit up the room and warmed that space in her center the way it always did.

Paul brought her hand to his lips and placed a featherlight kiss on her knuckle. "I'm going to make you love me again, baby."

Heat rose up her arm and tingled behind her neck. She might have sighed, she wasn't certain. Flashes of the two of them together, him touching her in places, kissing her in places… She blinked the images away but not the fire that raced through her veins and the longing that echoed in her soul.

* * *

They stood in front of Layne's car in the underground parking garage.

"Thank you for dinner."

"No, thank *you*—for listening." He cupped her cheek.

Her breath hitched.

"I want to kiss you," he whispered, drawing closer.

Heat flashed through her body. Her heart raced. She should turn away, push him away, but it was too late.

The familiar warmth of his lips touched down on her mouth and air stuck in her chest. He pressed, slowly, tenderly, parting her lips, testing the tip of his tongue along her mouth, in it, dancing until the glacier that she'd erected around her heart began to melt and her body grew soft and pliable.

Paul groaned. He snaked an arm around her waist; the other hand threaded through the twisted cotton of her hair.

Layne whimpered. Gave back and gave in. The time, the loneliness, the hurt peeled away layer by layer until she was exposed and yearning and vulnerable. She pulled away, stepped back, brought her hand to her thoroughly kissed month. She spun toward her car door, fumbled with the key fob. *Beep.*

"Layne, please. Wait," he gently urged. He lightly touched her shoulder, turned her to face him. "Don't leave like this. I didn't mean to push you. I…wanted to kiss you, to feel you again, but I can take it slow.

I can. I will. I'll do whatever you want, however you want to do it."

She'd seen all of Paul's personas over the years: the consummate professional, the thoughtful conversationalist, the loyal friend, the life of the party, the counselor, the artistic lover, but never this. She'd never seen him truly exposed and raw. It was in the pleading in his eyes, the urgency in his voice.

She pulled in a breath and slowly exhaled. "What you did to me by not thinking enough of me to help me get to where I wanted, hurt me in ways that I can't even explain. For all the time that we were together it was always the way *you* wanted things, the way *you* saw things. And when I finally did something for me, *you* couldn't handle it so *we* couldn't be. Then you come here—" she threw her hands up "—after all this time, and take that one thing that I wanted for myself. You say you love me. Maybe. You say you were an egotistical asshole. True. You say you want to make it right." Slowly, she shook her head and looked him in the eye. "I don't know if you can."

His head lowered.

"You have a lot of work to do, Paul." He looked up. "And unlike the millions that watch you everyday and gobble up your every word, I won't. If you want me, if you love me like you say you do, you're going to have to prove it. Kisses and sweet talk will not be enough." She pulled open the car door and slid behind the wheel. "Up to you," she added before shutting the door and turning on the engine.

She slowly pulled off. From her rearview mirror

she watched him standing there, fine as all get-out and totally put in his place. Layne smiled. *Now, let's see what you got.* She exited the lot and drove out into the warm summer night.

"Get. Outta. Town," Tina chirped as she and Layne strolled along M Street, stopping from time to time to check out a shop window. They each grabbed a cup of gelato, then continued on toward Wisconsin Avenue to check out the arts festival.

"Yes. I still can't believe it."

"But do you want to believe it is the question?"

Layne scooped a spoonful of gelato into her mouth, savored the sweetness. "I'm definitely not going to make it easy for him."

"I should hope not. Doesn't deserve it. Make him beg," she said wickedly.

Layne giggled.

"So." Tina lowered her voice and hooked her arm through Layne's. "Was the kiss as good as you remembered?"

Layne threw her head back and laughed. "Girl, I almost lost my natural mind. Another minute and no telling what I might have agreed to."

"What next?"

Layne gave a slight shrug. "Up to him. We'll see."

After having roamed through the street vendors displaying their art, Layne bought a brilliant abstract of a man and woman entwined on a meadow and Tina purchased a muted painting of four jazz musicians on stage.

Layne and Tina parted ways around three, with Tina saying she needed to get ready for a very hot date with this guy she'd met during a local journalists' conference. They were going dancing and she "needed a nap" before stepping out.

Layne returned to her apartment with the intention of taking a hot shower, ordering some takeout and reading Tiphanie Yanique's latest novel that she'd had on her to-be-read pile for months.

Just as she stepped out of the shower, her cell phone chirped. *It better not be some problem at work.* She grumbled as she padded across the bedroom floor. She picked up the phone and frowned.

"Hello?"

"Layne, it's Paul."

She dropped down on the side of her bed. "Paul—how did you get my number?"

"Your cell is on the call sheet, remember?"

She squeezed her eyes shut. *Of course.* She cleared her throat and crossed her bare legs. "Okay. And you're calling because...?"

"I don't want to waste one more minute for us. I'm sure you might have plans for the holiday weekend, but if you don't, I was wondering, hoping, that you'd want to take a drive out to Baltimore Harbor for the crab fest. I know how much you love the water and seafood. I thought it would be fun. Give us a chance to talk, spend time together. See the fireworks from the harbor."

She was silent.

"I'll do all the driving, going and coming. And I'll pay the tolls *and* gas."

She burst out laughing. "Fine. Okay."

Paul chuckled, too. "Great. I'll pick you up at about eight. The traffic will be crazy."

"We, uh, could leave tonight. Get a head start. Find someplace to stay." She swallowed. Her heart hammered. What the hell was she thinking? Too late now: The words were out, the gauntlet had been thrown.

"I'm...good with that," he stammered.

Layne wondered if she'd thrown him off by being so quick to accept his offer.

"I'll throw some things in a bag. Pick you up."

"I can check the hotels in the area..." She tugged on her bottom lip.

"Okay."

What was she doing? "Um, seven sound good?"

"Great. I'll see you at seven...if you give me your address."

She laughed and gave him her address.

"See you at seven," he said.

"I'll be out front." She hung up the phone before she really said something additionally crazy. She tossed the phone on the bed as if it was a hot poker and leaped to her feet, then spun around in a frenzied circle. What in the world had she just done?

You know what you've done. She went to her dresser and pulled open her lingerie drawer. *You know exactly what you've done.* She picked out three of her favorites: black, hot pink and virgin white. Would it be as good as she remembered? *It better be.* She shoved the drawer shut, then went to check on vacancies in Baltimore.

* * *

Layne had just stepped out the front door of her condo when Paul pulled up. She inwardly smiled with approval at his choice of vehicle. Mercedes GLS SUV in black. Hmm. Nice.

Paul hopped out, came around and took her bag. "All set?"

"Yep."

He opened the passenger door for her, then took her bag, opened the back hatch and put the bag inside next to his.

"You look great," he said, clearly nervous.

Layne angled her head in his direction. She bit back a grin and the impulse to say something snarky. Instead, she said a simple thank-you, knowing full well that an H&M T-shirt and biker shorts were not up there with Versace, but she'd take it. He was trying.

"I figure it will take about an hour and a half to get to Inner Harbor, straight up I-95." He tossed her a quick look as he slid into traffic heading to the highway. "So...did you find a place for us to stay?"

"All the hotels in the area were booked. But I found an Airbnb—a townhouse. We lucked out. The owner said there was a last-minute cancellation. We'd have the entire place to ourselves, and it's close to everything."

Paul smiled in admiration. "You always knew how to put a plan together," he said. "Remember when the station manager wanted to host a retreat for the staff and we arrived only to find out that the reservation had never been finalized?"

"Oh my goodness! Yes." She started laughing. "What a hot mess."

"You got on the phone, made some calls, twisted some arms and got us into the W hotel, *at* a discount." He chuckled. "Man." He glanced at her. "Same way you run your team with efficiency. No energy wasted." He pulled in a breath, switched the topic. "Some music?"

"Sure."

"Still love classic R&B?"

She grinned. "Is there any other kind? You still have your go-to playlist?"

"Is there any other kind?" he teased, holding her with a smile while he pressed the lighted panel on the console.

Martha Reeves and the Vandellas, classic "Heat Wave," pumped through the speakers and they immediately joined in, singing off-key and loving it, followed by "One Nation Under A Groove" by Parliament-Funkadelic, "Tracks of My Tears" by Smokey Robinson and the Miracles, and "Shining Star" by Earth, Wind & Fire.

For every song that came on they tried to out sing the other, their voices cracking over their unbridled laughter. Singing the R&B chart toppers was one of their Friday night activities, their very own at-home karaoke. They'd discovered early in their relationship that they loved the same music. What was crazy was that most of the music they loved had been popular before they were even old enough to talk. But it was their thing. They laughed and sang and reminisced for the entire drive.

After a few wrong turns they pulled up in front of the townhouse and hopped out.

Paul glanced up at the two-story redbrick structure tucked between similar buildings on either side, took in the quiet tree-lined street beneath a dusting of stars in a cloudless sky. He nodded in approval. "So far so good," he said with a wink, then opened the hatch and took out their bags while Layne tapped in the code that the owner had given her to unlock the front door.

They stepped inside, welcomed by the soft scent of lavender.

Layne flicked on the light. The squared-off foyer opened to a cozy living room with a redbrick accent wall and a fireplace. Simple but tasteful furnishings sat on gleaming wood floors. To the right was the kitchen that led out to a tidy backyard. On the opposite side of the living room was a small study.

"There are two bedrooms," Layne offered, "and an authentic claw-foot tub," she quickly added. "Upstairs."

"Cool." He bobbed his head. "I'll take the bags up. Guess you can choose which room you want your things in." He picked up the bags and headed upstairs, chortling James Brown's "Papa's Got a Brand New Bag," much to Layne's amusement. She followed him upstairs.

The spacious bedrooms with queen-size beds were situated on either side of the bathroom along a long hallway.

"I'll take this one," Layne said, stepping into the room closest to the staircase. Paul brought her bag in and set it down next to the club chair by the arched windows.

"You've outdone yourself, Layne. This place is sweet."

She turned to face him and images of them in his bedroom back in Charlotte floated in front of her. How many nights did she listen for his key in the door—the highlight of her day.

"Thanks. I think we'll be very comfortable."

"Speaking of comfort, we should figure out what to do about dinner." He patted his taut stomach.

Layne laughed. "Definitely. I'm going to freshen up a bit and I guess we can take a walk around, see what's available."

"Sounds like a plan." He turned away and walked to his room.

Layne sighed heavily, planted her hands on her hips and looked around. They would be there for the next four days. How long would they stay in separate rooms?

Arm in arm, they strolled along cobblestoned streets, paused and peered into shop windows, and made up outlandish stories about the people they passed on the street. They found a cozy, family-run soul-food restaurant and had the best chicken and waffles this side of Atlanta. On the way back to the townhouse, they stopped in an all-night mini-mart and loaded up on snacks, breakfast fixings, coffee and two bottles of wine.

Happy and a little tired, they tumbled into the living room and plopped down on the sectional couch.

"Nightcap?" Paul suggested.

"Sure."

He took a bottle of wine from the bag of groceries and went in search of two glasses.

Layne toed off her sneakers and tucked her feet beneath her. Paul returned with two glasses and a bowl.

"For the popcorn," he said in answer to her raised brow. He opened the bottle of Prosecco, poured two glasses and filled the bowl with popcorn. He sat a gentlemanly distance away on the couch.

Layne leisurely sipped her wine. "This was a good idea, I think," she said. She glanced at him, offering a half smile.

He studied her for a moment. "I think so, too." He glanced around. "I don't see a sound system. Want to watch a movie?"

"I'm fine. I'd just like to sit here for a few. Unwind."

He finished off his glass of wine and took a handful of popcorn. "You just relax. I'm going up to take a shower, get the day off of me." He smiled and rose to his feet. He placed the bowl of popcorn in front of her. "Good night," he said softly.

"Good night," she whispered back.

Once Paul was gone, Layne put down her glass, closed her eyes and leaned her head back against the couch cushion. If she had planned a perfect day, it would have been one like this. The drive was fun and easy. The townhouse absolutely perfect, dinner, the conversation, the walk through town…everything.

Paul. She pulled in a breath and sighed. Too perfect? Too easy? Was it real or did she simply want it to be?

In his presence, she felt better. The space inside her felt warm. But she was still struggling to wrap her mind around his reasoning for doing what he did. That was what gave her pause. That was what made her put on the brakes when it was so easy to go full steam ahead.

But the truth was, she understood Paul. He was driven. He had a big ego and his ego was what propelled him to achieve all that he'd done. He was rooted to his own principles, sometimes intractably so. But as much as those traits were a strength, they were also a weakness as they blinded him very often to how his actions and his vision conflicted with others, and they would not allow him to back down. In all the years that she'd known and loved him, she'd never seen him give in. He believed it was a weakness. *You have to stand by your convictions. If you give in on one thing you'll give in on something else*, he'd told her when they'd first met. *And before you know it, what will you have? What is a man without his word, his beliefs?*

So, based on what she knew about Paul, his confession to her about what he'd done and why he'd done it went against every fiber that made Paul Waverly the man he was. For him to break his own mantra, to leave his home and job, come to DC and ultimately undress his soul was a big deal, and the fact that he was willing to do whatever it took to win her back meant this was a brand-new Paul Waverly. A Paul Waverly she wanted to get to know in a new way.

She heard the doors overhead open and close. She sighed deeply and rose to her feet. It was almost midnight and she and Paul had talked about getting an early start to get over to Inner Harbor for a full day. She really wanted to visit the National Aquarium while they were in Baltimore. She'd heard about it since she'd relocated to DC, but had yet to visit.

She went upstairs. Paul's bedroom door was shut, but she heard the faintest strains of music. She guessed he was listening on his phone. She gathered her toiletries and headed into the bath. For a moment she debated about a shower or a soak in the magnificent claw-foot tub. Ultimately, she opted for the shower. She'd save the deep soak for tomorrow. She was sure that with all the walking and touring and shopping they'd planned she would need it.

Finished, refreshed and actually revitalized, she stepped out of the bathroom and right into Paul's path.

"Sorry. Was going downstairs. Thought I'd top off the night with one more glass of wine," he said, staring at her. "Couldn't sleep."

Layne inhaled the fresh-washed scent of him—remembered it. Her heart raced.

"You're beautiful, you know," he said, his voice low, almost awed. His eyes moved over her face, down to the opening in her robe and back.

Her breath hitched. He reached out and tenderly moved a wet tendril of hair away from her face before cupping her cheek. Her eyelids fluttered close.

"Layne," he whispered. "I need you..."

She glanced up at him to the familiar love and longing in his eyes and knew that the last vestiges of her resistance were falling away. Her robe parted when she lifted her arms to drape around his neck and melted into him when he swept her flush against the hard contours of his body.

His groan vibrated in the center of her chest when his mouth covered hers in a searing kiss. Her tongue mated with his in a slow, sensual dance that sparked flames of desire.

He brushed her robe from her shoulders, kissed her collarbone, trailed his lips up her neck and across the shell of her ear. Her body shuddered with hunger.

Her robe pooled at her feet. She clutched the end of his T-shirt and tugged it over his head, tossing it to the floor. His head dipped to the swell of her breasts and he buried his face between the firm pillows. Her neck arched. She gasped as his mouth encircled a taut nipple.

Paul lifted her into his arms and pushed open the door to his bedroom. Layne was dizzy with need, the images of his room fuzzy around the edges.

In long strides he crossed the room and laid her down on his bed. For several moments he stood above her. Her gaze hungrily drank him in.

"Is this what you want?" he asked, his voice almost hoarse.

"Yes," she whispered. "Yes."

Paul pulled off his khaki shorts and kicked them to the side.

Layne sucked in a breath, taking in the beauty of him, and the memories of the feel of him inside her flooded her senses. She sucked on her bottom lip with her teeth as Paul lowered himself down beside her.

They turned on their sides to face each other.

"I love you, Layne. I never stopped loving you."

Paul captured her mouth, kissed her long and deep as his hands smoothed across her waist, her hips. He hooked his arm beneath her thigh and draped it over his waist. His throbbing erection pressed against her belly.

Her fingers threaded through the tight coils of his hair, trailed down his neck and kneaded the ropes of muscle in his back.

They took their time exploring, remembering, reconnecting, yet it was all new and thrilling.

Paul eased her onto her back and braced his weight on his forearms. He placed featherlight kisses on her lips, then her cheeks, her throat, and down between the valley of her breasts. He cupped her breasts in his palms and brushed his lips back and forth across the warm skin, nipping and suckling, teasing as she moaned and writhed beneath him.

He moved in maddeningly slow degrees down her body until he reached the heat between her thighs. Layne sucked in air from between her teeth. Paul placed a hand on each thigh and gently spread them wider. Layne gripped the sheets in her fist.

His tongue flicked back and forth across the tip of her clitoris. Layne cried out. Her hips arched. Paul cupped her rear in his palms and brought her to his mouth.

"Ohhhh!" Her inner thighs trembled. Flashes of electricity shot up her limbs.

Paul was expert and thorough, bringing her to the brink of release time and again until she begged for him.

"Tell me what you want," he urged. "Tell me."

"You," she moaned.

He moved above her. She wrapped her legs around his waist and felt the pressure of his erection press against the welcoming wet heat. The air stuck in her chest as he pushed across the threshold. Paul groaned, and she cried his name. That instant when they became one was surreal.

What was thought to be lost became familiar again as they found their special rhythm, moving in undulating waves that ebbed and flowed through them, carried by their moans and sighs of pleasure. Hands and mouths explored, teased and urged. The sounds of desire only intensified along with the thrust and arch of bodies.

The tips of Layne's fingers pressed into Paul's back, her thighs tightened. Paul's thrust quickened, deepened, and his breathing grew ragged. Layne's moans rose until she was crying out as wave after wave of pleasure poured through her, shook her. She arched her hips. Paul pushed harder, faster. He held her hips in a steely grip. His head fell back and a guttural groan rose from his gut as the months and months of longing for the woman he loved exploded in mind-shattering satisfaction.

Their heaving breaths mixed and mingled and bubbled into joyous, giddy laughter.

Paul tumbled over onto his back. Layne looped her leg across him and curled against his side.

"You're off to a good start proving yourself, Mr. Waverly."

Paul angled his head, looked into her eyes and grinned. "And I have all the proving you need." He leaned over and sealed his promise with a kiss.

The rest of the days and hours spent together during their long holiday weekend getaway was pure magic. They laughed and talked and debated, sang, ate and toured the city, watched the fireworks, made love as often as humanly possible and tumbled head over heels back in love with each other.

It was their last night before driving back to DC, and Layne finally decided to make use of the claw-foot tub. Paul was puttering around in the kitchen with promises that he was going to prepare a great snack for the movie they'd rented and planned to watch.

Layne slowly slipped into the steamy, scented water and let out a satisfied *ahhh* when the water reached just below her chin. She leaned her head back against the pillow attached to the lip of the tub and closed her eyes. Her skin prickled from the heat.

The past few days were directly out of a perfect romance novel. *"Handsome, sexy, intelligent man sweeps reluctant, stubborn, independent and sexy woman off her feet in a whirlwind weekend escape. Will the dashing hero be able to capture the heroine's questioning heart?"* She smiled as she took a mental inventory of her body, running her hands along the wet dips and curves, noting all the tingles, tenderness and electric energy that coursed through her. If capturing the heroine had any connection to conquering her body, then all was lost for the feisty heroine. She giggled. But even so, as with all romance novels, our heroine could not let the hero think he'd won just yet.

The bathroom door eased open. She opened her eyes and turned to see Paul with nothing on but a thick towel wrapped around his waist and carrying a tray in an awful parody of a waiter.

Layne sputtered a laugh. "What in the world are you doing?"

"Your snacks, madame." He made a perfunctory bow.

"You are nuts." She giggled.

Paul crossed to the tub, pulled a small stool next to it and placed the tray of assorted cheese and crackers and red and green grapes on the stool along with a bottle of wine and two paper cups. He set the bottle of wine on the black-and-white tiled floor.

"I am here to serve, madame," he said with another mock bow. He unknotted the towel and let it drop to the floor.

Layne sucked in a sharp breath. No matter how many times he'd done it before, seeing him naked in full display always took her breath away.

"I think madame might be in need of a massage and I believe I can help." He smiled wickedly and eased into the hot water behind her. "Hmm, this is nice," he murmured into her damp hair. He reached for a grape and brought it to her mouth. With his other hand he roamed the rise of her breasts beneath the water, sliding smoothly across skin made slick and supple from the hot, scented water.

A cracker this time while he moved lower, across her belly that fluttered beneath his fingertips. He kissed the back of her neck, nibbled her earlobe, tweaked her nipples. Another grape while his hand moved between her bent knees and stroked the wet folds until she began to moan softly and slowly undulate her pelvis against his fingers. He brushed her mouth with the tip of his thumb and she sucked it in between her lips.

His erection pulsed against her. A finger slid inside her. She gasped. Arched. His palm cupped her breast, squeezed gently. Moans. Breath heightened. Her hand covered his, pressing, urging him deeper.

"I want you," he whispered hotly in her ear. "Now."

He stifled his groan in the hollow of her neck, suckling her there. She cried out. Her hips rose. Two fingers. Heat. So hot. Her toes curled. In and out. Faster. Nip on her neck. The quickening deep inside.

"Paul! Paul!"

"Come for me," he groaned in her ear, flicked his thumb across the pulse of her swollen clitoris, and her limbs stiffened as a bolt of electricity shot through her, then shook her as her wet inside sucked on the source of her pleasure.

"Ohhhh, ahhhh!"

"Yesss," he whispered. "Come for me."

When the last wave of her release subsided, she sank against his chest, weak but utterly satisfied. That had been so damned good she wanted to cry.

Paul kissed the back of her neck and tenderly caressed her belly. Her insides fluttered, came to attention. It couldn't be possible that she could want more, but she did and after all she owed it to Paul, who obviously still had needs to be met.

She maneuvered her body so that she was astride him. He hummed deep in his throat, brushed her hair away from her face. "You're beautiful, you know that?" He kissed her, full and deep.

Layne slid her hand down between them and stroked him. His breath hitched.

"Look at me," she demanded.

Paul opened his dark eyes that had grown darker with lust. Long, steady strokes from hilt to tip. His nostrils flared. His head lolled back. He sucked air between his teeth.

Without missing a beat, Layne rose up on her knees, positioned his very hard shaft between her legs and slowly descended until they were sealed together.

Paul's fingers dug into Layne's hips, preventing her from moving until he'd gathered himself enough not to explode on his first stroke.

She lifted up her breasts in her palms. Paul leaned in, took one tip between his lips, sucked and teased and then the other. Layne's neck arched back. She tried to rock her hips against him. Finally, he released her and rose up high and hard inside her. Not to be outdone, she rode him with abandon. Water splashed them, spilled onto the floor, stirring up a whirlpool that spun them, captured them then tossed them into the throes of release.

Later, winded but utterly satisfied, Paul murmured, "Who's gonna clean up the mess?"

Layne took a sleepy-eyed peek over the edge of the tub. "Oh my goodness."

They broke into laughter.

The drive back to DC was much different from the trip going. Now they held hands along the way, shared smiles and secret glances. They laughed more, and the initial awkwardness of being together after being apart for so long was gone. There was a renewed intimacy between them and an afterglow from their loving that hung around them like an aura.

But the closer they drew to DC and home, the more the reality of their new situation began to settle and become the third passenger in the car.

"So, um, how are we going to do this?" Layne finally ventured.

Paul inhaled deeply. "I've been thinking about it." He gave her a quick look before steering onto the entrance of I-95. "I don't want it to be like last time. Secrets and sneaking around."

"So, what are you saying?" She licked her lips. Her heart thumped.

"I'm saying that I don't want us to hide. That doesn't mean making out in the hallways or having blow-your-mind sex on top of your desk or the supply closet." He gave her a wink. She smacked his arm. "But not being afraid of being seen together. Know what I mean?"

She was thoughtful for a moment. "I get it. And I'd like nothing more than to be out in the open." She paused. "But I don't want anyone thinking that I somehow got the producer spot because of you. And—" she twisted her body to look at him "—I still want to sit behind that desk, Paul. I worked for it, I earned it. That hasn't changed. I'm a damned good producer but I know I will be a phenomenal anchor."

His brows flicked. "Where does that leave me, us?"

She sighed and looked away, then back at him. "Your contract is for six months. I'll produce the best damned news show you've ever been a part of—my way. At the end of six months we'll talk about next steps as a couple and as professionals."

"Damn, woman, you drive a hard bargain." He chuckled, snatched a look in her direction. "Deal."

"Besides, that will give you plenty of time to perfect your 'proving it to me' routine."

"I think I was off to a pretty good start this weekend, if I have to say so myself," he said with humor in his voice.

"I'll have to do some…comparisons in the coming days, weeks and months," she teased.

"Ready, willing and able."

Seven

"So, I'll see you tomorrow at work," Paul said. He'd parked in front of her building.

"Yes. Tomorrow." Should she invite him up? No. They needed a bit of distance to clear their heads. She opened her door.

Paul hopped out and grabbed her bag from the back and helped her out. They faced each other.

"I'm going to miss waking up next to you. It got easy real fast," he said, looking into her eyes. He placed a kiss on her forehead. "Tomorrow."

She swallowed. "Tomorrow." She turned and tapped in the security code and the front door buzzed open. She dare not look back because her resolve would be nonexistent and the next thing she knew she'd be making breakfast for him in the morning. She pressed the button for the elevator. This weekend was only a test. They were definitely sexually compatible. The real test would come in the days ahead when sex wasn't the answer, and the blush of the weekend had begun to fade.

She turned the key in the lock to her apartment door in harmony with the buzzing of her cell phone. She pushed the door shut with her foot, tossed her keys in the bowl that sat on the table by the door and fished her phone out of the back pocket of her jeans.

She looked at the name on the screen and snickered.

"Damn, Tina, are you stalking me or what? You see me come in the door?" She dropped her bag next to the living room couch and kicked off her sneakers, then plopped down.

"Look, I gave you the weekend. I didn't bug you for details. I 'let you live,' as the kids would say. But my sistah, time is up and I am itching for details. And if you are *just* getting back then you have some stories to tell."

Layne dropped her head back against the cushion of the couch and shut her eyes a moment. Flashes of Paul above her, beneath her, around her popped in her head. She shook it to clear the images and to calm the tingle that was blooming—again. *Damn!* She crossed her legs.

"Listen, I am literally just getting in the door. For real. Give me an hour and come on by. We'll order Chinese."

"No. Had Chinese last night. Mexican. And make it a half hour. See ya."

She hung up before Layne could protest. Layne shook her head and laughed, then pushed up from the couch and went to empty her carry-all.

* * *

"Say what now—in the tub?" Tina squealed. "Damn, I always wanted to do that." She bit down on a piece of quesadilla and chewed thoughtfully. "Hmm, have to be a good-sized tub, though."

Layne snickered. "We did more than have great sex," she qualified with a lifted brow.

"Could be, but that's the fun part." She took a long swallow of iced tea. "But on a serious note, how are you feeling, and what are you thinking with regard to you and Paul?"

Layne released a slow breath. "Being with him this weekend reawakened what I thought was dead and buried. I was reminded why I fell in love with him, but also reminded why I left. The crazy thing is," she continued, "before, back in Charlotte, it was Paul calling all the shots—the how and when. Now it's me. I'm going to do what's right for me. I'm hoping that it all works out, that Paul and I will walk through this together. But I know I'm not going to take a back seat to anyone else's vision for me. Whether I'm in love with him or not."

The work vibe on the team was decidedly different in the ensuing weeks. The undercurrent of tension between Paul and Layne had dissipated and the positive results were evident with the crew. They felt more free to speak up during briefings, and most noticeable was that rather than debate or shoot down Layne's story ideas, Paul seemed to champion them. Deanna noticed as well and made it a point to check in with Paul on a regular basis to see how things were going.

* * *

Paul returned to his office after signing off. It had been more than two months since the getaway. In between they were spending time with each other on the weekend, in and out of their respective apartments, dinners, museums and the theater, but Paul wanted more. Layne said she wasn't ready.

He shrugged out of his jacket and hung it on the back of his chair. The desk phone rang. He snatched up the receiver.

"Waverly."

"Paul, it's Deanna. I was hoping you could join me for dinner."

"Dinner?"

"Yes. Is that a problem? I thought we could talk about the future. Your future."

He cleared his throat.

"I thought I'd order in and have it brought to my office. I have a bunch of meetings today. Does seven work for you?"

How could he say no? In the time that he'd been there, Deanna had been promoted from executive producer to program director in charge of daytime and nighttime news programing. She held the keys.

"Seven sounds fine."

"See you then."

Paul returned the receiver to the cradle and leaned back in his chair. He ran his hand across his face and heaved a sigh. In the past couple of months, Deanna had inserted herself more and more into the day-to-day activities of the *Morning Show.* Where before he'd been the one that made life difficult for Layne, for which he'd made amends, it was now Deanna that seemed to go out of her way to pinprick Layne, nixing her story ideas, questioning her decisions.

He and Layne talked about it, curled together beneath the sheets. Layne was growing concerned and had begun to question Deanna's motives. It was almost as if she wanted her to fail, Layne had confessed, to get rid of her for reasons that she couldn't put her finger on, not to mention that she felt that Deanna had a thing for him. He tried to reassure Layne that Deanna was simply trying to assert herself in her new position and was eager to prove to the higher ups that they hadn't made a mistake. But as much as he tried to allay Layne's misgivings, he was beginning to feel uncomfortable with the direction things were going with Deanna: the phone calls, after-work texts, invitations to meet for late lunch after the briefings. Hopefully, tonight some things could get straightened out, but with Layne already feeling a bit off-center about Deanna's "designs" on him, the last thing she needed to know was that he was having dinner with Layne.

His cell phone chirped with Layne's text.

I'm heading home. Will I see you later tonight?

He stared at the phone, then typed his reply.

Not tonight, babe. I'm gonna turn in early. Tomorrow?

Sure. Tomorrow. Get some rest.

Will do.

Love you. He mouthed the words but didn't text. A wave of guilt rolled through him. He'd make this dinner thing with Deanna quick and efficient, voice his concerns and get the hell out of there.

"Thanks for coming," Deanna greeted. "Come on in." She held the door open. "I've sent everyone home so that we can talk in private," she said, lowering her voice conspiratorially and placing a hand on his shoulder.

Paul forced a tight-lipped smile. He glanced at the circular conference table that had been set up for dinner complete with white tablecloth, a bottle of wine and several silver-covered platters.

"You didn't have to go to all this trouble. I'm not really hungry."

"Don't be silly." She guided him to the table. "A man has got to eat."

He pulled in a breath and walked to the table and sat in the nearest seat.

"Wine?" She held up a bottle of something very expensive.

"No, thanks. Water is fine." He poured a glass of sparkling water into his glass. "You said you wanted to talk about the future," he began, cutting to the chase.

"My, my, can't we at least have the salad first before we talk business?" She lifted one of the silver covers, revealing a beautiful mixed green salad with all the trimmings. "Help yourself."

Paul filled a glass salad bowl and slid it toward him. Deanna did the same and took a seat to his right.

"When we met at that conference…one, two years ago—" she wagged a slender finger at him "—I knew you were the one. Something special. And I would do whatever I could to get you here." She lifted her glass of wine and took a short sip. "I pulled a lot of strings and called in a lot of favors to make that possible. But you know that," she said with a dismissive wave of her hand. "And you have not been a disappointment. So far."

"I have a good team and a great producer."

Her cheeks darkened. She licked her lips. "But lately," she continued, "you haven't been the sparkling star that you were when you arrived."

Paul frowned. "What do you mean?"

"You've gotten soft around the edges. The past couple of months. You haven't been the same. The fierce anchor is coming across too touchy-feely."

"I don't think so. I deliver the news and interview my guests the same way I always have."

"I'm thinking it's time to shake things up a little. Sweeps are coming up in November. We have two months to make sure that we shine."

"What do you mean, shake things up?"

"Well, I want to reassign your producer."

His jaw clenched. "Why?"

"Layne Davis has talent, behind and in front of the camera. I want to give her some time to do for nightly news what she's done for *The DC Morning Show*, and give her some more air time. It's what she's always wanted. Isn't it?"

"You would know better than I do," he said. His mind raced.

"Did the two of you work closely back in Charlotte?"

"No. We didn't."

"Hmm. So what do you think?"

Now he wished he did have a drink. "I think you're making a mistake."

She got up from her seat and sidled next to him. She sat on the edge of the table. "I don't make mistakes. That's why I'm in the position that I'm in. And I intend to keep that track record in place. I have senior VP of the network on my bucket list." She rested her hand on his shoulder and leaned closer. Her voice dropped an octave. "We'd make a formidable team, you and I."

"I thought we already did."

She smiled. "This is nothing compared to what we could do together, *really* together. I could take your career to the next level. You could be a real shot caller—with my help."

He stared up at her. The green of her eyes sparked like emeralds.

"Your dinner's getting cold," he said, then pushed back from the table and stood. "And I really have to go."

She got to her feet and pressed a hand against his chest, halting him. She stepped closer, gripped the lapels of his suit jacket. "Think about my offer, Paul," she purred, leaned in and kissed him full on the mouth. No friendly peck but one filled with longing and power.

He stepped back. Her cheeks were flushed, her eyes simmering.

"Good night, Deanna." He brushed by her and half expected the door to be locked, like in one of those bad B movies. He flung the door open and stalked out.

He went through every variation of expletive known to man on his way down on the elevator. His temples pounded. He knew seeing Deanna after hours had been a bad idea, but like an idiot he'd done it anyway. And what was worse was that he'd lied to Layne about where he'd be.

He went to his office and actually locked the door behind him, then went to his private bathroom to throw some water on his face. He looked in the mirror and his mouth was streaked with her red lipstick.

"F—" What if someone had seen him? He scrubbed the lipstick away then checked the collar of his shirt and his jacket.

This could go left a million different ways. Deanna was a very influential, power-hungry woman and there was no telling what she might do if crossed. He sure as heck couldn't report her. Who would believe him? Best to keep this to himself and play it by ear.

He took one last look in the mirror, pulled out his cell phone and pressed the speed dial button.

"Hey, baby. You know what, I really want to see you. The heck with going to bed early." He forced a laugh. "About an hour."

He made love to Layne that night as if it was the first and the last time all rolled into one. With every stroke, he promised, with her every cry of his name he promised, and in the silence when they held each other in the dark he promised to be everything that she needed.

"So, what are you going to do, man?" Paul's brother Eric asked.

Paul paced the floor of his living room, then went to stare out the window. "I don't know exactly." It had been about two weeks since that dinner rendezvous. So far Deanna hadn't done anything about moving Layne, but he knew it was coming.

"Sounds like this Deanna can make major trouble. You have some protections because you're her star player, but if she's trying to get with you and thinks Layne is in the way, Layne is the one that will come out on the short end of the stick."

"Hmm, yeah, I know." He paused a beat. "My option is still open at WNCC," he said quietly.

"Meaning?"

"I could cut my losses, protect Layne, go back to Charlotte…"

"And you'd be right back where you started—hundreds of miles away. Didn't work before. Piece of advice…"

"I'm listening."

"Tell Layne the truth. Don't let her get blindsided. You won't be able to recover from that."

"You're probably right."

"I know I'm right. Take it from a married man.

Women know stuff. They just do. I don't know how, but it's like a freaking superpower."

Paul chuckled. "I'll tell her." He held his phone away from his ear and looked at the time. "I'm going to pick her up for dinner in about an hour. We haven't been out together in a while. I'll tell her everything tonight."

"Public places are always best," Eric said tongue in cheek. "Less chance for a scene."

"Gee, thanks."

"Good luck, bruh. Let me know how it goes."

"Thanks and I will. Tell Tricia hello for me."

"Will do. Later."

Paul disconnected the call and went to take a quick shower.

The weather was exceptionally warm for late September. The streets of Georgetown were still lined with people in the outdoor seating of the numerous cafés; couples and families strolled leisurely along the cobbled walkways, and the Galleria Mall was teeming with shoppers and tourists. Strains of music could be heard floating out of the doorways of the jazz clubs and bars. All very typical for a Saturday night in DC.

Parking was pretty much nonexistent on the weekend, so Paul opted for an Uber. The car dropped them off in front of Blues Alley Jazz on Wisconsin Avenue NW. Blues Alley was famous for its live shows with some of the greats as well as aspiring performers.

"Thought we'd do something a little different tonight," Paul said as he helped Layne out of the cab. "I have reservations for the nine o'clock performance. Thought we could sit outside a while, see the passersby, have a drink before dinner and the show."

"I'm all in." She smiled and leaned in to kiss him.

He slid an arm around her waist and pulled her close. "I was hoping you'd say that," he said.

She leaned her head on his shoulder while they waited for a table to be cleaned and set up for them.

A cab eased to a stop, waiting for the red light to change. Paul did a double take when he thought he spotted Deanna. She briefly turned in his direction but before he could be certain the cab pulled off across the intersection. He thought to mention it to Layne but shrugged it off. He was probably wrong.

Paul held Layne's chair while she sat down. They ordered a plate of calamari to share and two glasses of wine.

"To us," Paul said, raising his glass.

Layne tilted her head to the side. "To us." She tapped her glass against his and took a quick look around. "Funny, I've been living down here for three years and this is the first time I've been to Blues Alley. I was always promising Tina I'd go with her, but I'd wind up being the third wheel so I always turned her down." She sipped her wine.

"You didn't date, have anyone special?" he tentatively asked. He never wanted to imagine her with anyone else, but he would be a fool to think that she'd been totally alone.

Her gaze rose to his for an instant, then away. "Not really. No one special. I went out from time to time—"

she gave a slight shrug "—but I was and am focused on my career." She forked a piece of calamari and dipped it in the sauce before popping it into her mouth. She chewed thoughtfully. "I never asked about your love life after…us."

He pursed his lips a moment. "Not much to tell. I was in and out of relationships, no one long-term."

Layne looked down at her plate. "So no one special?"

"No. No one." He reached across the table and covered her hand with his. "The truth is I didn't want anyone but you, but I was too stubborn to admit it. And the more time that passed, the harder it became. The offer to come here was the ticket I'd been needing. So I took it."

Layne sighed softly.

The waitress came to take their dinner order. They both ordered blackened catfish with red beans and rice.

"As much as I love us being together again, I have to be honest with you."

"Go on."

She hesitated. "You being here basically ruins whatever chance I might have had to anchor the show." There, she'd said it. The feeling that had been hovering in the back of her mind since he arrived was fully out in the open.

She might as well have slapped him. Although she cared for him, might even love him again, there was a part of her that resented him, no matter the reason for his actions.

"But," she pushed out a breath, "I'm dealing with it. I'm actually enjoying being a producer, more than I thought I would. And I'm damned good at it. I get the best of both worlds, working on the show and seeing you every day." She smiled.

"I only want you to be happy. And if me being here is taking away any part of your happiness—"

She cut him off. "It's not. It's not," she repeated.

The waitress arrived with their meals.

"Wow, this looks delish," Layne said.

"Babe, I need to talk to you, tell you some things."

Her fork of catfish stopped midway between her plate and her mouth. "Okay. Sounds serious." She teased the fish off the fork with her teeth, chewed slowly. "I'm listening."

"Remember that night a few weeks back when you asked me to come over and I said I was going to turn in early?"

She frowned. "Yes. But then you came over anyway."

"Yeah, there was a little more to it than what I told you."

She put down her fork. Her eyes flashed. "Whatever it is, just say it." Her tone was a mixture of demand and apprehension.

"I was invited to dinner with Deanna, in her office, alone."

"Say what?"

He held up his hand. "Please just hear me out."

Layne listened in silent hurt and fury, until Paul's

confession and Deanna's plans were laid out on the table between them.

The only thing she said when he was done was "You lied to me."

"It was stupid. I didn't want you worried or upset. I—"

"You lied to me. Then you slept in my bed and made love to me as if nothing happened." Her breathing escalated. "If you could do that..." She tossed her napkin on top of her plate. She fished in her bag for her phone.

"Wait, what are you doing?"

"Calling an Uber. Maybe her little plan is all for the best. We do need to be away from each other." She pressed the app and scheduled her ride. "If she moves me to nighttime I'll gladly take it to be away from you. Because if you lied about something like that, what else would you lie to me about?"

"Layne, you have this all wrong."

"You know what, I don't care."

"It was never my intent to lie to you. I should have told you."

"Yeah, you should have told me. Then."

"I didn't and I'm sorry. You have to believe that. Layne, I love you. I didn't mean to hurt you. I was trying to protect you."

She pushed to her feet, checked her phone and then the street. Her car was pulling up. She blinked back the sting of tears. "Like I said, I don't care." She spun away and quickly walked to the waiting car. She took one look back, got in and slammed the door shut.

* * *

Layne and Tina sat side by side on a bench in Rock Creek Park that Sunday afternoon. Fall was definitely on the horizon but the last vestiges of Indian summer were holding on tight.

Layne pulled her sweater around her. "I just don't know what to think anymore."

"I have to admit, Paul can be a real screwup when it comes to doing the right thing in the relationship department, but do you really believe that he intended to do something *with* Deanna?"

"I don't know. No. Maybe." She blew out a frustrated breath.

"Do you have any space in that big brain of yours to believe that what he said was true, that he was only trying to protect you and figured he could handle things on his own?"

Layne stared off at a pair of kids chasing each other around a tree. "What he did was messed up. Without a doubt. I could probably get beyond that, but what bothers me deep in my soul is that he lied. Not so much after the fact—by omission—but before. He knew he was going to see Deanna when he talked to me and he intentionally lied. It wasn't as if it was some spur-of-the-moment thing." Her frown deepened. "That's the part I can't wrap my head around," she said with resignation.

"I get it. Believe me. Men are not always the brightest."

They both snickered.

"Well," Tina said on a breath, "I can't tell you want to do. You know what you want and you know what's in your heart. At some point Deanna is going to move you to late night with the intent of eventually getting you in front of the camera—where you wanted to be. If you can find your way clear to see past Paul's latest screwup then maybe things can work out. Or not." She flashed a crooked smile.

"You are so not helpful." She patted Tina's thigh and got to her feet. "Let's see what's on the brunch menu at Mom and Pop."

"I thought you'd never ask."

For the next two weeks Layne focused on producing her program and keeping thoughts of Paul as far at bay as possible. Unfortunately, it was extremely difficult to ignore the secret glances he tossed her way when he thought no one was looking or the apology texts that she ignored.

Maybe she should have followed his urging in the beginning and come out front with them being a couple. Maybe none of this would be happening if she'd done that. When she thought about it, it was like what Yogi Berra said: "It's like déjà vu all over again."

She was just finalizing the storyboard for the week when Cherie burst into her office without knocking.

"Did you hear?" Her voice was frantic.

"What?"

"Security just escorted Paul out of the building."

She dropped her iPad. "What? What are you talking about?"

"I was coming back from lunch and I saw it with

my own eyes. Everybody is buzzing about it, but no one has any facts."

Her brain was on scramble. She pressed a hand to her forehead. "What the—"

Her desk phone rang. She flashed Cherie a glance and answered. "Yes. Okay. I'll be right up." She hung up the phone and looked at Cherie. "Deanna wants to see me."

Cherie cussed.

Layne slid her cell phone into the back pocket of her jeans and picked up her iPad.

"What do you think happened?"

"Haven't got a clue, but I'll tell you all I know as soon as I find out," Layne said, opening the door to her office. Her thoughts raced. "And don't feed into any rumors," Layne warned before walking out.

The elevator doors opened onto the executive level. Layne walked up to the reception desk.

"Ms. Mitchell asked to see me."

"Ms. Davis. Yes. You can go right in. She's waiting for you."

"Thank you." She turned and walked down the carpeted corridor to Deanna's new office now that she was program director. She knocked lightly.

"Come in."

Layne walked in. Deanna was seated behind her desk, impeccable as always. She glanced up from the pages in front of her, smiled tightly and extended a hand toward the chair in front of her desk. Layne sat down and had the unsettling feeling that she was facing a firing squad.

Deanna slapped the cover of the folder shut and linked her long fingers together. “I’m sure you’ve heard about Paul.”

“Not exactly. What happened?”

Deanna lifted her chin. “He’s been suspended pending an investigation.”

“Investigation? For what?”

“I’m not at liberty to say. It confidential.”

“For how long? And what about the program? This is crazy.” She shook her head in disbelief, her thoughts flying in a million directions.

“The length of suspension will be as long as it takes for the investigation to conclude. And as for the program, I am promoting Cherie to producer, and you will sit in Paul’s seat beginning tomorrow.”

She blinked in confusion. “What?”

“It’s what you’ve always wanted. I’m sorry this is the way you got it. But, this is a trial run. We’ll see how you do. Get us through the sweeps. I think having a woman behind the desk is going to take us to the next level. Don’t you?”

Layne gripped the arms of the chair. She felt as if she’d been tossed into some alternative universe. What was happening?

“I’ll want to meet with you and Cherie to discuss the handoff. In the meantime, go down to Wardrobe. They’ll get you all set up.”

This was all surreal. Deanna was going on as if upending an entire program, ousting the lead and rearranging a stellar production team was something that happened every day.

"Of course, if you have any concerns, I'm always here." She smiled brightly. "But I don't expect that there will be." She flipped the folder back open.

Mindlessly, Layne rose from her seat.

"I know you will do great. It's what you've been working so hard for. Now it's all paying off."

Even as the words sounded like a compliment there was a viciousness to them that floated just beneath the surface.

"You can leave the door open," Deanna said, her attention already diverted.

Layne retraced her steps down the hallway and back to the elevator. The doors swished open and Cherie stood there.

"What happened?" she asked in a harsh whisper.

"We'll talk. Come to my office when you're done." She stepped into the elevator just before the doors closed.

As soon as she returned to her office, Layne called Paul. It went straight to voice mail. She sent a text. No response. He was probably in a state of shock, she thought, her heart aching for him.

What could possibly have happened? Deanna was a piece of work but this was crazy. One minute she was your strongest ally, the next she would cut you off at the knees. This was the second anchor in less than a year who'd been dismissed. Was she next on the chopping block? She rested her forehead in her palms.

The rest of the day was a frenzy of activity, between speculation, staff upheavals and general uncertainty. Layne met with Wardrobe to plan out her outfits for the rest of the week, and she'd called an emergency staff meeting of her team for the end of the day.

All she wanted was for the day to end so that she could go over to Paul's place and find out firsthand what had happened.

Her team was gathered in the small conference room next to the control room. The buzz of speculation was palpable.

"I'll get right to it," Layne began. "Management has made some major changes. As you all know, Paul Waverly has been suspended." She held up her hand to forestall any questions. "That's all I know. I don't have any other details." She tugged in a breath. "Per the program director's plan, I will take over the anchor spot and Cherie will step in as producer."

There was a hum of voices. "This is going to be a big transition for all of us and I expect that you will give your all to Cherie the same as you did for me."

"Of course."

"For sure."

"Cherie has already been briefed on what to do, and she will bring you all up to speed. Thank you, everyone, for all of your hard work and support. We'll get over this hump together. Remember we have sweeps coming up and we can't afford not to be on the top of our game." She smiled. "But going forward, I'll leave the pep talks to Cherie. Thanks everyone."

Layne walked out sad, scared and excited all at once.

She left the building, got in her car and went straight to Paul's building. She went to the concierge's desk and asked him to ring Paul's apartment.

"Sorry, Mr. Waverly left a couple of hours ago."

"Oh, um, he didn't happen to say when he'd be back? It's about work. I've been trying to reach him."

"I'm sorry miss, I have no idea. He didn't say. He did have a suitcase with him."

Layne frowned. "Oh. Okay. Thank you." She turned away. Where would he have gone? She tried his cell again. Voice mail.

"Wow, Layne, that is some kind of crazy. You still haven't been able to reach Paul?" Tina asked.

"No. I've left at least a dozen voice messages, not to mention texts. No response."

Tina tucked her leg beneath her on the couch. "I hate to say this, sis, but my mama always told me to be careful what you wish for."

"What's that supposed to mean?" she snapped.

"It's like making a deal with the devil. Sometimes the thing you think you want comes at a cost."

Layne rolled her eyes. "That just makes me feel so…much better." As much as she hated to admit it, there was a glimmer of truth in what Tina said. She'd been fixated on the damned anchor seat at the expense of everything. Now she had it, but it was only because it was taken away from Paul, the man who'd given up what he cherished for her.

Where could he be?

If he didn't stop along the way it was a solid six-hour drive to Charlotte. He could make it by ten, eleven at the latest. When he'd called his brother, Eric, to tell him he was driving down, Eric had insisted that he stay with him and Tricia, at least for tonight.

He wasn't sure what to make of what had happened this morning. He'd come in early as usual and there was a message on his answering service that he was to go to HR immediately following the end of his show. A call like that from HR was never a good sign. But maybe it was no more than firming up the last few months of his contract. The last thing he'd thought was that he would be unceremoniously escorted from the building, his credentials taken and advised that allegations had been made against him and until a thorough investigation was complete, he was suspended.

Hours later, he was still dazed by the whirlwind of events, trying to make sense out of them. *Allegations.* God, that only meant one thing in this climate. His phone buzzed in the cradle. It was Layne. Again. He dismissed the call. He didn't need to talk to her, not now. He believed that somehow Deanna was behind this, but he just didn't know to what degree.

By the time he arrived at his brother's house, his head was pounding and every bone in his body ached.

“Tricia roasted a chicken for dinner. Kept a plate warm for you in the oven,” Eric was saying as he walked with his brother into the house. “Figured you’d be hungry.”

He snorted a laugh. “I actually am. Haven’t eaten since this morning.”

“I’ll get us set up. Figured I’d wait ’til you got here and I’d eat with you. You know where everything is. You’ll be in the guest room.”

“Thanks, bruh.”

“Hennessy?”

“You know me too well.”

“Coming right up.”

“Hey, Paul.” Tricia came downstairs. “I thought I heard you.”

“Didn’t mean to wake you.”

“Not at all. I was waiting for Jimmy Fallon to come on.” She grinned. “Kept dinner for you.” She came up to him and kissed his cheek.

“Thanks.”

“Okay. Good night, fellas.” She gave her husband a leisurely kiss and a squeeze of his arm. “See you in the morning.” She turned around and went back upstairs.

Paul walked down the short hallway to the guest bedroom on the right. He flicked on the light, looked around and for a moment wondered how he’d gotten there. Gotten to this place in his life. Deanna Mitchell. She had the power to ruin everything he’d built for himself, and for what? She might have wanted him, but not because she actually cared, but because she could and somehow believed it was her right to have what she wanted.

He set his bag down near the foot of the bed and went to the bathroom to wash up so that he could join his brother for dinner and a drink and maybe make sense of it all.

Layne had dozed off on the couch. Something woke her. The sound of sirens in the distance. She sat up and craned her stiff neck, then immediately checked her phone, hoping for some word from Paul. Nothing.

She unfolded her body and slowly stood. She considered trying Paul again, but thought better of it. Wherever he was, it was clear that he didn't want to talk to her and she had a big day coming up. Her heart ached.

Layne had stepped down from her duties as producer and worked with Cherie to get up and ready. Whispers still ran rampant about Paul Waverly. *Oh, how the mighty have fallen*, some said. Others joked that the anchor chair had become a hot seat and who knows how long Layne would last before she was kicked to the curb.

Cherie stepped into her new role and responsibilities with ease, having learned all she needed to know by being Layne's right hand. Now Layne had to call on her experiences in front of the camera and deliver.

Be careful what you wish for. The old mantra echoed in her head as she took her seat behind the anchor desk and watched the signals for her cue.

"*The DC Morning Show* with Layne Davis."

Her red light went off.

"Good morning. I'm Layne Davis here in our studios in downtown DC. At the top of the news today from Capitol Hill…"

The two-hour segment went off without a hitch. Layne quickly found her footing and Cherie's setups were perfect. The entire team rose to the occasion and gave themselves a well-deserved round of applause when the technical director announced, "And we're out."

After one of the assistants came to un-mic Layne, she crossed the studio floor, stepping over the snaking cables until she got to the control room.

"Great job, everyone. Thank you for making my job easy."

The remaining team gave her a thumbs-up as they geared up for the next program following the local weather. Layne went in search of Cherie, but was stopped in the hall by Deanna.

"Layne, just who I want to see."

"Everything okay?"

"I watched your debut today. Impressive. I should have given you the shot long before now and we wouldn't be in yet another mess," she said, lowering her voice. She looked her over. "You might want to do something with your hair. Maybe you can smooth it out some. For a more polished look." She tossed off a tight smile and walked away.

Layne absently patted her twisted locs that she'd styled into a topknot and muttered a curse, then spun away.

Eight

The aroma of fresh-brewed coffee wafted into his room and stirred him awake. He blinked against the light streaming in from the window. For a moment, he was disoriented. Then his reality sunk in and the events of the day before came crashing back.

He groaned and pushed up to a sitting position, tossed the blanket and sheet aside and got out of bed. After taking care of morning rituals, he padded into the kitchen.

The house was quiet. It was almost nine. It was the first time he'd slept this late on a week day in longer than he could remember. He must have been more tired than he'd realized. There was a note on the table in his brother's familiar scratch.

"Fresh coffee. Full fridge. Help yourself. Had an early day. We can talk tonight. E."

Paul smiled, crumbled the note and tossed it in the trash. He filled a mug of coffee and went into the living room. He turned on the television and scrolled through the news cable stations until he found WWDC. He drew in a breath.

The News at Sunrise was concluding, followed by three commercials and a weather update. And then the logos for *The DC Morning Show* filled the screen.

"Good morning. I'm Layne Davis..."

Paul sat up. His pulse ticked. He stared at her, in his seat, the one she'd always wanted. She was good. Damned good. He smiled, but by degrees his smile faded.

What was really happening? Layne gets her dream job on the back of his suspension. Was Layne behind this alleged complaint? Did she lobby for the job? Deanna would have been more than happy to stick it to him since he wouldn't play ball.

The more his mind twisted around the unthinkable scenarios, the more enraged and confused he became. He turned the television off, returned to his bedroom, got dressed and went out for a walk to clear his head.

He walked about three blocks, picked up a newspaper along the way and stopped in a neighborhood diner. The waitress said he could sit anywhere, so he took a seat at a small square table in the back. The laminated menu boasted a French toast special, complete with two eggs any style and sausage links or patties.

The waitress arrived with a carafe of coffee. She turned the coffee cup over and filled it without asking. “Morning. Know what you want?”

“I guess I’ll go with the special. Scrambled eggs and links.”

“Coming right up.”

He nodded his thanks and opened the paper, started from the back at the sports section and worked his way forward. He’d just bypassed the arts and entertainment section and was settling on international news when the waitress returned with his breakfast.

“Here ya go, sir. Can I get you anything else?”

“No, thanks. I’m fine.”

“Well, you just let me know.” She paused, studied him for a moment. “Didn’t you use to be that news guy? Paul. Paul Waverly!” She snapped her fingers. “Used to come on in the mornings. It is you!” She beamed as if she’d just found something she’d lost. “Can I have your autograph?”

“I…sure.”

She shoved her order book at him. “Sylvia. You can make it out to Sylvia.”

He scribbled his name and thanks to Sylvia and handed it back.

She held it to her chest. “So what happened to you? I don’t see you on the television anymore?”

Paul swallowed. “Thanks for breakfast, Sylvia.”

She flushed. “Oh, I’m sorry. Didn’t mean to pry. It’s just that…well, you enjoy your breakfast. Let me know if you need anything.”

He turned his attention back to his meal, reached

for the syrup and lathered his French toast. Between bites of food he absorbed the headlines and latest details on the war, the shakeup at NATO, and the growing threats of domestic terrorism. He ate up the news as thoroughly as he ate his breakfast. This was what gave him a rush, purpose. The idea that he might not be able do what he loved shook him. Sure, he could go back to WNCC—maybe. He still had time on his option to return. But if word got back as to why he'd been suspended from WWDC—whether true or false—those doors would close as well.

He sat back and glanced around. *"Didn't you use to be...?"* The waitress's words played back in his head. Would that be his legacy?

He folded the paper, pushed his plate aside and put a twenty-dollar bill beneath the coffee cup. It should be plenty to cover breakfast and maybe the waitress would have a story to tell about how that *guy who used to be* left her a nice tip.

He stepped out into the slightly overcast morning. Soft gray clouds moved across the horizon. He stood for a moment, undecided what to do next, feeling suddenly adrift as if the anchor of what stabilized him had been lifted. He began walking. What he did every day mattered. It mattered not only to his audience but to him as well. It was who he was. And now it seemed he didn't have Layne, either. Without Layne, without being able to do what he loved—who was he? He was just that guy who used to be.

Light drops of rain began to fall. He picked up his pace and headed back.

* * *

"So this suspension just came out of the blue?" Eric asked as he and Paul sat on the enclosed back porch sipping beer.

"Totally did not see it coming, especially after all Deanna did to get me to come to DC, in the first place." He paused a minute, debating whether to share his dark thoughts with his brother. But if not with Eric, then who? "You know, this morning I watched the news. Layne has my spot."

"Oh." Eric frowned.

"When I saw her at first I was excited. She was great. But then I went down this dark hole. Like did she engineer all this? She never hid the fact that she was laser-focused on getting that seat."

Eric's head jerked back in incredulity. "You're kidding, right?"

"Now I am. But not this morning. I guess I was still in shock to be sitting on the couch and not behind the desk, and then to see Layne...knowing that's what she wanted all along..." He exhaled. "I lost it for a moment."

"I sure as hell hope you found it. You know that is all the way in left field, bruh. Layne may be as ambitious as you but she wouldn't slip behind you and stab you in the back."

"Yeah. I know. Momentary lapse."

"She know you're here?"

"No. She's been calling but... I'm not really ready to talk about it. Need some time to decompress. Get my head on straight."

The brothers were silent for a moment.

"What happened to the last guy that had the spot?" Eric asked.

"He was let go after an investigation."

"Any idea what it was about?"

"Not really. There was some talk about misuse of corporate credit cards or something. Some say there were *allegations*." He took a long swallow of his beer and pulled the hood of his sweatshirt over his head. "I never met him, so I have no opinion and didn't want to start my tenure off by getting involved in office gossip."

"I'm only asking, as an attorney, to see if there are any patterns going on here."

"Patterns?"

"Yeah, dismissals that follow a similar track."

"I wouldn't really know."

"It's something that I would want to look into, if it comes to that. What exactly is the accusation against you?"

"Inappropriate behavior against a colleague."

"Could they be more vague?" Eric scoffed. "Well, I'm going to want to see the actual complaint."

"I don't need you getting involved," he said, waving off his brother's offer.

"I *am* involved. I'm your brother and I'm not going to see you get railroaded."

Paul leaned his head back and closed his eyes. In a meandering way, that was totally not how he ever presented information, he tried to tell his brother about his apprehension about his future. "Layne. My work.

They make me who I am. You know I was a mess when she left."

"Yeah, and were too stubborn to admit it. You could have made it work if you didn't let your big head and ego get in your way."

"I thought you were on my side," he groused.

"I'm on the side of right. Look, one thing that I've come to terms with is that we can't be defined by just one thing—our career, where we live, how much money we make, who we love. Sure, we're a sum total of all those parts and over time some of those parts shift and change, disappear or are replaced. But that doesn't make us any less than who we are—inside. Because the key piece of who we are is what we are inside, the kind of human beings we are, how we treat other people. That's what really matters, bruh."

Paul lowered his head and smiled. "When did you get all wise and whatnot?" He glanced askance at his brother.

"Man, I been wise and whatnot. Mom always said I had a smart mouth." He winked.

Paul sputtered a laugh. "Yeah, okay."

The brothers sat back, staring up at the clear October sky, dusted with stars and a quarter moon.

"You should call her," Eric said quietly.

"I will as soon as I figure out what my next moves are going to be. This time when I come to Layne, it needs to be with a clear plan, a clean slate, no strings and total commitment. I don't feel like myself right now and I want to be in a good space and clearheaded before we talk. There's been enough confusion, secrecy and uncertainty between us for too long—overshadowing everything else. This time I want to do things right."

Eric lifted his bottle of beer. "I got your back."

"Thanks, bruh."

Lying in bed, he held his cell phone up to his face. He was hoping that there was a message from Layne, but there wasn't. She hadn't called or texted all day. He started to call her, then stopped. He wasn't ready. The one thing that he didn't share with his brother was the real reason holding him back from calling Layne: He was ashamed, embarrassed. He'd always been "the big man on campus," the star, the one everybody looked up to. He'd bought into his own hype, and now with the rug pulled out from under him, he realized just how shallow he'd become. That was not the man he wanted to present to Layne. And he wouldn't make any moves in her direction until he was sure of his footing.

Layne was in her office when Cherie knocked.

"Come in."

"Hey, you did great today," Cherie enthused and plopped down in the armchair.

"Thanks. And you stepped into those producer shoes like a champ." Layne grinned.

"We need to go have a drink and celebrate."

"I'd love to, but my first day took a lot more out of me than I thought. I'm going to head home, review my notes for tomorrow and turn in early."

"Sure. I get it. I guess I'm still running on adrenaline." Cherie pushed to her feet. "Did you hear anything official about Paul? How long is the suspension? Is he coming back?"

Layne stomach knotted. "I don't know. I haven't heard anything."

"Hmm. Okay." She stood. "See you in the a.m., and Layne?"

"Hmm?"

"I never got to tell you how much I appreciate you mentoring me and giving me this major break. No matter how things go, I'll still be able to put producer on my résumé. I have you to thank for that."

"You deserve it, C. I wouldn't want anyone else."

"Well, just know that I appreciate it." She went to the door. "See you in the morning."

The moment Cherie was gone, Layne checked her phone to see if she'd missed a call or text from Paul. Nothing. She sighed. It had only been two days. He probably just needed his space. But if she did not hear from him by the end of the week, it was gloves off.

Layne and Tina met up at their favorite after-five spot. Tina wanted to hear every detail about her debut and the latest on Paul.

When they were seated after a short wait, they put in their drink orders. Two frozen margaritas.

"So, how was it? How do you feel?" Tina urged.

"It was…amazing. The thrill was beyond what I imagined. It flowed, I didn't screw up my lines, hit all my cues. Cherie did an amazing job. Handled it like the pro she is. Made my job easier for sure."

Tina leaned in. "I am so happy for you, sis. For real. As long as I've known you this has been your dream."

The waitress arrived with their drinks.

"Thanks," Tina said. She turned her attention back to Layne. "Was it worth it?"

"Meaning?"

"Don't get me wrong. You have talent from here and back and all roads in between, but your victory was a result of someone else's loss. Someone that you love."

"What are you saying? That I don't really have what it takes? That I'm there by default?"

"Not at all. But what I am saying is that no good comes from benefitting from the fall of someone else." She held up her hand to halt Layne's protest. "What I want you to think about is how sketchy this all is. First Deanna is your bestie at work, a big cheerleader. But she hires Paul for a job she knew you wanted. Then she begins to undercut you. Then out of the blue 'allegations' are lodged against Paul and, poof, he's gone and you're in. You said yourself that you thought she had a thing for Paul and he admitted what she did in her office."

"I didn't want to believe that Deanna orchestrated everything. But she wanted Paul from when she first met him. She saw an opportunity to bring him to DC, but when he wasn't as 'grateful' as she wanted, he's out, and puts me in his spot to rub it in his face."

Tina arched a brow in agreement.

Layne sipped her drink. "Have to find a way to prove it."

"That's why you have me as a best friend," Tina said with a smile.

Layne finished out her second week and still no word from Paul. Deanna stopped by after every show to compliment Layne and offer unsolicited advice.

"What is the status with Paul?" Layne asked after the final show for the end of the week.

"I'm sure he won't be back."

"Has the investigation or whatever was going on finished?" she asked.

Deanna's eyes narrowed. She waved away the question. "I would concern myself with my own job if I were you." She gave Layne one last look. "Enjoy your weekend." She turned and walked away.

Layne sighed. What was her objective? Was she so obsessed with her own power that she simply got rid of anyone that got in her way or didn't give her what she wanted? Paul had told her what happened that night in Deanna's office. She'd been hurt and angry, so much so that she didn't allow herself to see beyond her own feelings to what was really going on. Deanna caused the toxic environment and anyone in her way paid the price.

In the meantime, Tina had assigned one of her investigative journalists to do a follow-up with WWDC and a full exposé on the history of the station. It would take weeks, Tina cautioned, but she was certain they would get to the truth.

Layne couldn't wait for the journalist to finish their work. She needed to talk to Paul, face-to-face. There was one thing she knew about Paul and that was he was a creature of habit. She was going to take a chance and drive to Charlotte.

Layne went straight home, packed a bag and was on the road within the hour. She didn't have a plan other than finding Paul. She'd figure it out when she got there.

She crossed into Charlotte a little after nine. Now that she was there, she wasn't sure where to look first. It was too late to start knocking on the doors of old friends. She'd have to find a place to stay for the night and start fresh in the morning. She drove into the center of town, better known as Uptown, and remembered the Grand Bohemian Hotel, a boutique hotel that had great rooms, wonderful service and sweet memories.

"Welcome to the Grand Bohemian. Do you have a reservation?"

"No. I don't. I just got into town and I was hoping that there was something available."

"How long will you be staying?" the reservationist asked as she keyed information into the computer.

"Um, just for the weekend."

"I have a room available on the second floor. Queen."

"I'm sure it's fine. Is room service still available?"

"Until eleven."

"Thanks." She handed over her credit card.

The reservationist returned her credit card and a room key. "The elevator is around this corner on your right."

"Thank you."

"Enjoy your stay."

Layne took the elevator and proceeded down the quiet hallway to her room. As she'd expected, it was just as she remembered.

In the early days of their relationship, she and Paul had spent a getaway weekend here. At the end of a workday, he'd found her in the break room, and checking to be sure no one could hear him, had whispered that he had a little surprise for her and that she should go home, pack a bag and he'd pick her up at six.

The Grand Bohemian Hotel was where he'd brought her. They'd had dinner in the hotel restaurant, lounged on the rooftop patio, swum in the pool and spent the rest of the weekend making love and ordering room service. When they finally emerged on Sunday afternoon, their commitment to each other was cemented.

Layne stripped out of her clothes and took a long shower, then ordered room service. While she wolfed down her burger and fries, she scrolled through her contacts on her phone. She was pretty sure she had Paul's brother's contact information.

There it was! Hopefully, his number had not changed.

She would reach out to him first thing in the

morning. If anyone knew where Paul might be, it would be Eric. Before she settled down for the night, she called Tina to let her know she'd arrived safely and her plan to reach out to Eric. Much to her satisfaction, Tina informed her that her journalist was making some alarming discoveries and that she would keep her posted.

Layne barely slept and was up with the sun. She fixed a pot of coffee and waited a reasonable time to text Eric. At 8 a.m., unable to wait any longer, she typed her message.

Hi, Eric. This is Layne Davis. I was hoping you could tell me where I could find Paul. He hasn't answered any of my calls or texts. I'm here in Charlotte. Please get back to me. Thank you.

She stared at her phone, waiting for the tiny bubbles to appear to indicate that he'd received her message and was answering. More than an hour went by without a response.

If she didn't hear from him, her next move would be to visit the station. Hopefully, some of her and Paul's old colleagues had seen or spoken with him. Then again, he might not be in Charlotte at all. She should have thought this through before being so impulsive and driving all this way.

Then her phone chirped. She snatched it up from the bed and saw to her relief that it was Eric.

I'm glad you reached out. Paul is actually staying with me and Tricia. I'm not home at the moment. I had to come into my office, but call back around six and I'll pass the phone to Paul. I told him he needs to talk to you, but you know how my brother can be.

Thank you so much! I will call at six.

She exhaled a long breath of relief. He was here. She would speak to him tonight and they were going to work things out one way or another. Six o'clock couldn't come fast enough.

She went down to the hotel restaurant and had breakfast before taking a walk to think and take in the sights of the place she'd once called home.

The funny thing about the Queen City was that while other places referred to their central business district and hub of activity as Downtown, it wasn't so in Charlotte. Its main area of commerce, entertainment and culture was called Uptown.

It had been almost four years now since she'd been back. Much of what she remembered was the same. There were a few more coffee shops and a vegan café that she didn't recall, but for the most part Charlotte remained unchanged.

She strolled along N. College Street and stopped for a moment to take in the sculpture of Queen Charlotte, the city's namesake, before continuing to the Four Corners Statues at the intersection of Trade and Tryon Streets and was happy to discover that the Bechtler Museum of Modern Art was just opening for the day. On their last night at the Grand Bohemian years earlier, Paul had taken her to the museum for a jazz night that took place in its massive lobby. Even though by that time they'd discovered they both loved classic R&B, jazz tied for first place.

They were taking a chance that they might be seen by someone who recognized him from television or the both of them from work, but that night they didn't care, even though Layne wore a hat and Paul kept the hood of his sweatshirt on all night—just in case.

She smiled at the memory. It was such a magical weekend. The direction of their relationship had shifted from teasing and tentative to purposeful. Even though they had to navigate the landmines of company politics and the power dynamic of Paul's position, they'd found ways to make it work until it didn't. Was it all worth it?

On her way back to the hotel, Tina called.

"Were you able to reach Paul?"

"I got in touch with his brother, Eric. Paul is staying with him. Eric said to call tonight at six and he'd put Paul on the phone."

"Well, I have some news that you can share with Paul, but it can't go any further until we confirm some more information."

Layne pushed through the lobby doors and found a cozy corner out of others' earshot and sat down. "What is it?"

"It seems that Deanna Mitchell has a shady history with the men at the station."

"Meaning?"

"Meaning that these so-called allegations were all smoke and mirrors to get rid of anyone that she'd set her sights on but they didn't reciprocate. If you get my drift."

"What?"

"Yes."

"In other words, Paul is not the first."

Layne's thoughts swirled. "How has she been able to get away with this?"

"Nondisclosure agreements upon hiring. We've uncovered at least five. And it seems that the board turned a blind eye because she kept churning out great programming."

"Wow," Layne said on a long breath. "So, now what?"

"Now we keep digging until all the pieces are in place and any unanswered questions are resolved."

"Man, this is like freaking Watergate."

Tina snickered. "Lights, Action, Scandal. Talk to you later. Let me know how it goes with Paul."

"Thanks, T. Really."

"I got you."

Tina's revelations spun around her head. How long had this been going on? Was Deanna that narcissistic that she would ruin someone's career just to satisfy some misplaced sense of power? Six o'clock couldn't come fast enough.

She hadn't brought anything special to wear. The best she could come up with was a white cotton pullover sweater and black slacks. She'd always had a penchant for sexy underwear, so that wasn't an issue—*if* things got that far. So she spent some extra time in the shower and arranging her hair.

With nothing left to do but wait, she curled up in the chair by the window and kept checking her phone for the time.

When 6 p.m. popped up on the screen, she hesitated. She didn't want to seem too anxious and call on the dot. She waited a painful ten minutes, then dialed Eric's number. He picked up on the second ring.

"Hi, Eric. It's Layne. Is he there?"

"I'll go get him."

"Did you tell him I was going to call?"

"Nope. Didn't feel like hearing him tell me how I'm in his business," he said with a chuckle. "As if that would matter. Hang on."

Layne heard muffled voices. Her heart was pounding so hard and fast it was difficult to breathe.

"Layne…"

His voice was like water after a drought. It flowed through her, nourished her. She felt as if the dry leaves of her heart were beginning to bloom again.

"Hi," she breathed. "How are you?"

"Hard to say," he admitted. "One minute I'm good, the next… How are you? I miss you," he added before she could respond.

Her heart thumped. "I miss you, too. We have so much to talk about. Did Eric tell you that I'm here, in Charlotte?"

"What? No. You're here?"

She giggled. "Yes. And you'll never guess where I'm staying?"

"Where?"

"At the Grand Bohemian."

"Our first getaway," he murmured.

"Yes," she said softly. "A lot of good memories. I thought maybe you could come by here and we could talk over dinner."

"I'd like that. I can be there in about an hour. That good?"

"I'll meet you in the lobby."

"See you then."

"Okay."

"And Layne—"

"Yes?"

"I'm glad you're here. See you soon." He disconnected the call.

She held the phone to her chest, closed her eyes and smiled.

Layne felt like a nervous teen on a first date as she waited for Paul in the hotel lobby. Her goal was to look cool and collected when he came through the door but that didn't stop her pulse from jumping every time someone pushed through the revolving doors.

She was about to check the time again on her phone when she felt him before she saw him. Her head snapped up and something warm and satisfying filled her, brought her to her feet. He came straight for her and as if they were the only ones in the world,

Paul took her in his arms and kissed her as thoroughly and as hungrily as a man starved.

Their lusty embrace drew smiles and murmured comments from the comers and goers.

"I think we might be causing a scene," Layne whispered breathlessly against Paul's lips.

"I don't care."

She tossed her head back and laughed, a pure, joyous sound.

"I'm sorry, baby." He cupped her cheek. "Sorry."

"So am I."

He kissed her again, then slid his arm around her waist. She curled into his side, looked up at him. "Good to see you."

He kissed her forehead. "If I remember correctly, I think the restaurant is down the hall to the left."

"Yep."

They walked hugged up together to the restaurant and were seated at a table near the rear, and placed their drink orders.

Paul immediately reached across the circular table and took Layne's hands the instant the waitress walked away. "How have you been?"

"Okay. Stressed. Worried about you."

He lowered his gaze. "It wasn't fair of me to lock you out." He shook his head. "It was a major blow about the job. I didn't see it coming, and what happened between us about Deanna…me not being upfront." He blew out a breath. "I needed to take a step back." He paused. "And when I turned on the television and saw you in my spot, my first reaction was how great you are and how proud I was of you. But—"

"But then you started to think *how convenient*. It was what she always wanted and maybe—" she pursed her lips a moment "—maybe she might have had a hand in the fiasco." She looked him right in the eye and released a slow breath. "To be honest, I probably would have thought the same thing. But then reality would kick in." She smiled. "And we'd know better."

"Yeah," he said softly. "We'd know better." He lifted her hand to his lip and kissed it.

The waitress returned with their drinks and took their dinner orders.

"None of it was out of the blue," Layne said, lowering her voice. "Tina assigned a reporter to do a deep dive on Deanna Mitchell and the dismissal record at WWDC."

"And?"

The waitress brought their dinner.

"Thank you," Paul said.

Layne took her time to explain as much as she could based on what Tina had told her.

Paul's brows rose. "I knew Deanna was over the top at times, but this?" He stared at Layne.

"I know. Tina said there's still some loose ends to tie together but they should have a full picture soon."

"Hmm." He nodded and cut into his steak. "What about us?"

Layne angled her head to the side. She ran her tongue along her bottom lip and leaned forward. "I thought that maybe if you had some time, since I'm in town, maybe we could rekindle some memories."

A slow smile moved across his face. "Hmm, I'd love to help you remember. And start some new ones."

Layne dramatically raised her hand. "Check, please."

"Nice digs," Paul teased when they entered Layne's room.

She turned the door lock and engaged the security latch. "There's some wine in the mini-fridge." She took off her shoes.

Paul poured two glasses of white wine. He stood in front of her, handed her a glass. "To making new memories."

"New memories," she whispered.

They sipped their wine.

Paul nipped the glass from Layne's hand and placed it on the nightstand. He held her face in his hands. "Thank you for not giving up on me, for being the fierce, unstoppable woman that I've always known you to be."

"I love you," she whispered. "I fought against loving you as hard as I fought for all the other things I thought I wanted. But what I discovered is that at the end of the day, when I come home alone, none of it meant anything, because you weren't a part of it. I want us in this thing together, really together."

"So do I." He leaned down and kissed her tenderly at first, and by degrees with more urgency.

Layne leaned into him, looping her arms around

his neck, savoring the feel of his mouth, his tongue slow-dancing with hers.

His fingers threaded through the intricate twists of her hair until they came undone and tumbled to her shoulders. He broke the kiss and took the hem of her sweater in hand, pulled it over her head and tossed it to the floor. She laughed and returned the favor, expertly unbuttoning the tiny blue buttons of his Oxford shirt and tugging it off. He unzipped her slacks. She shimmied them off her hips and undid his. The corner of his mouth curved upward. His lids lowered when Layne reached in between the folds of his shorts and wrapped her hand around his stiffening member. He drew in a sharp breath and throbbed beneath her touch. Layne pressed her lips against his chest and covered it with hot kisses as she continued to stroke him. He groaned deep in his throat as Layne's kisses trailed lower. He gripped her shoulders and pulled her upright. His gaze scoured her face before his mouth captured hers, backing her toward the bed.

They tumbled onto the bed, sinking into the thick down comforter.

Paul peeled out of his slacks and shorts, unhooked Layne's teal-colored lace bra and matching panties in a series of seamless moves until they were both naked and heated with longing. His lips, his tongue, his fingers teased and paid homage to every inch of her body, making Layne writhe with desire.

Her soft moans rose in pitch as he kissed the inside of her thighs, stroked the tender skin with his tongue until the muscles fluttered. He pressed his mouth against her wet center and laved the sweet folds with his tongue until she begged him to stop, but he wouldn't, not until the orgasm that she tried to keep at bay rocketed through her, the force so strong that Paul had to grip her hips to slow her thrashing and allow him to bring her to total release.

Layne's soft whimpers and trembling slowly subsided. Her fingers that had been pressed into his shoulders loosened as Paul seductively moved up her body until he hovered above her.

"I want you," he groaned, his gaze boring into hers.

"Show me how much," she said, wrapping her legs around his back.

He leaned across her and grabbed his pants, took a condom from his wallet and put it on without wasting a beat.

When Paul eased inside her, filling her, sealing her body and soul to his, nothing else mattered except the two of them loving and giving of themselves to each other.

Layne lifted and rolled her pelvis to meet and invite Paul's every thrust: slow, fast, building in intensity. Their hard, quick breathing, moans and slap of bare wet skin filled the moist air.

"Paul! Oh, yesss. Yesss." Her body shook.

Paul scooped her body tight against his and exploded, deep inside her.

And much like during their first rendezvous at The Grand Bohemian, they spent the rest of the weekend ordering room service and making love.

Nine

"I'll keep you posted on anything I hear from Tina," Layne said, as she and Paul stood next to her car. "You could come back with me," she said with an inviting smile.

He leaned down and lightly kissed her lips. "That would be so easy, but let's stick to the plan." He braced her shoulders, looked her straight in the eyes. "This is important what we're doing, not just for me but for everyone at the station."

Layne nodded in agreement. "True." A slow smile bloomed on her face. "I was getting used to waking up next to you again."

"So was I."

She dragged in a breath. "I better get on the road. I have an early day tomorrow."

He opened her car door and she slid behind the wheel. He leaned in and kissed her. "Drive safe. Call me when you get in."

"I will."

"Love you," he whispered.

"Love you right back."

Paul pushed the car door shut and watched her car drive away until he could no longer see it.

"Well, the prodigal son returns," Eric teased when Paul walked through the door.

"Very funny." He dropped his backpack by the door and joined his brother in the living room. He flopped down on the couch and stretched out his long legs. "Where's Tricia?"

"Book club meeting." Eric shrugged. "So, how did things go? I mean, they must have gone well since you've been gone for two days." He chuckled. "But did you two get any dialogue in?"

"You're just full of jokes today. And yes, we talked. Thank you very much."

"And?"

Paul leaned forward and rested his arms on his thighs. He looked at his brother. "Man, some real shady stuff has been going on at that station and Deanna Mitchell appears to be orchestrating it. According to what Layne's friend that works for the *Washington Post* has uncovered…"

As Paul laid out what he knew so far, Eric began to pace, running his hand across his head and grunting under his breath with each revelation.

Eric blew out a breath. He looked at his brother. "We usually hear about this kind of stuff coming from men wielding their will and power on women and subordinates. This is a new twist."

Paul nodded slowly. Eric continued, "If everything you told me pans out, the station is going to have a lot of explaining to do. I'm pretty sure they will do whatever they need to keep it as hushed as possible." He paused a beat. "In the meantime, if you haven't done it already, you need to put as much of what you experienced—dates and times—on paper. You might need it."

"You're right. I'll corroborate events with my calendar."

"Good. Now—" he slapped his thighs "—I was going to put a couple of steaks on the grill. It's a nice night out, and when Tricia has her book club, all the sisters bring food, so a brother is on his own for dinner."

Paul chuckled. "Steaks sound like a plan. Let me get cleaned up and I'll help."

The brothers rose.

"It's really good having you here," Eric said sincerely, "and even better that you worked things out with Layne. She's good for you. She makes you better."

"I know. She really does."

Layne was exhausted from the six-hour drive but exhilarated at the same time. The past few days spent with Paul had cast all doubt aside about the viability of them being a couple. They talked, really talked about their fears, their hopes and the role that both of them played in their relationship splitting at the seams. But they committed above all else, no matter how hard it was, to be honest and transparent with each other. And to accept the fact that both of them might want different things at different times and that it was okay. They would find a way to work through it instead of walking away.

Back home, she stripped out of her road-weary clothes, took a quick shower and checked the fridge for something quick and easy to fix, and was sorely disappointed. Everything worth eating was frozen. As she debated whether to find something easy to defrost and cook or order in, the choice was, thankfully, taken out of her hands.

The front doorbell rang. She pressed the intercom. "Yes."

"I was hoping you'd be home by now."

"Girl! You have spies or what?"

"Buzz me in. We need to talk. And I brought Chinese."

Over shrimp fried rice, dumplings and egg rolls lathered in hot mustard, Tina explained what her reporter had determined. The sources were verified and they planned to publish the story in a matter of days.

"Deanna Mitchell has used sexism and intimidation against any man that either challenged her or didn't give in to her advances. There are six verifiable victims."

Layne felt sick to her stomach with the revelations. She knew what she had to do.

"This is how it's going to go down," Layne said and began laying out her plan.

She returned to work as usual on Monday, completed her program without a hitch or a hint of what was to come in the ensuing days. Paul was also making plans on his end and Tina said that the article would be ready to go the following morning.

"We need to talk," Layne said to Cherie once the show wrapped.

"Sure. Everything okay?"

"It will be."

"Okay. Give me ten minutes. Your office?"

"Perfect." Layne walked off toward her office. She caught a glimpse of Deanna getting on the elevator and rolled her eyes in disgust.

As promised, Cherie knocked on Layne's door ten minutes later.

"You have that determined look in your eyes," Cherie said when she came in. She took a seat. "What's going on?"

"Tomorrow we will have the programming the way you set it up. However, I will interrupt for breaking news."

Cherie frowned. "Breaking news that you already know about?"

"Yes. I don't want to say too much now. But I wanted you to know not to freak out when I go off script."

Cherie's brows rose.

"There will be fireworks and major fallout. I don't want you caught in the crossfire. The less you know the better. At least for now. I promise, I'll explain everything as soon as I can."

Cherie grinned. "This is so cloak-and-dagger! I love it and I trust you. Always have. I'll follow your lead."

"Thanks, Cherie."

"For you, anything. Hey, hear any updates on Paul?"

"Um, no."

Cherie looked at her for a moment. "Okay," she said on a breath. "See you tomorrow." She gave her a thumbs-up.

Layne offered a tight-lipped smile. "Tomorrow," she whispered in concert with the closing door.

Alone now, Layne momentarily wondered if what she planned on doing was the right thing. It would undoubtedly tank her career at the station and perhaps elsewhere. She might be perceived more as someone willing to stir up trouble rather than a dedicated journalist and professional. Tina had confirmed that the story would run digitally in the morning and the full details would be in print the next day and a full spread on Sunday.

Her pulse quickened. Of course, once the cat was out of the bag, every news outlet worth their credentials would be on it. She had to be ready to answer questions about her own hiring at the station as well. The one saving grace was that Deanna hadn't advocated for her in the first place and had never gone out of her way to champion her rise at the station until Paul. If anything, it seemed that Deanna had kept a lid on Layne's progress up the ranks, especially with regard to her desire to work in front of the camera—which was why she'd come to WWDC in the first place. It was ultra important, Tina said, that this did not appear as some kind of vendetta by a disgruntled employee. And it was also good that Tina had assigned the story to one of her reporters and had no hand in what had been uncovered. In hindsight, Layne realized it had been a smart move to not make her relationship with Paul public. That would only be fodder for more speculation in the wrong direction.

Most important, the article was not a hatchet job. It was transparent and did not shy away from naming names where necessary.

Layne drew in a slow breath. She was as ready as she could be.

Her goal was to get a good night's sleep so that she would look fresh and alert in the morning. However, she spent most of the night staring into the dark and listening to her heart pounding. When she pulled herself out of bed, her eyes felt gritty and her body ached as if she'd overexercised.

After a long, hot, pulsing shower and two cups of coffee, she felt more human. The stylist and makeup artist would fix everything else.

When she arrived at the studio, she stopped at the security desk to leave specific instructions that she was to be notified when her guests arrived and that they should be escorted to the studio immediately.

She went in her office to check any last-minute emails and verified that she didn't miss anything on her phone. Then she went to hair and makeup. Much to Deanna's great annoyance, Layne had opted not to tame her natural hair but to glorify it. Each day she showcased her natural twists in intricate patterns, and that had become just as much her signature as her direct delivery of the news at hand. Viewer feedback had been mixed at first, but then the tides seemed to change and the viewers applauded her embrace of her Black womanhood and the positive symbol that she represented. She would miss all that, she mused as Stacy the hair stylist coiled her hair into an elaborate top bun, leaving a handful of strands draped along the right side of her face. She'd wanted to be like her idol Cynthia Medley and carve out a path for other Black female journalists to follow. But she was pretty sure that after today, her chance for that would be at an end. Funny, but she was kind of okay with that. Because today was the kind of day that she'd worked toward for her entire career, breaking that major story that would reverberate and cause change. So if today was going to be her last day, she would go out with a bang.

Today she wore a simple sleeveless navy dress with a scoop collar and a chunky wooden necklace in a muted orange.

She had her notes in a folder, but before walking

onto the set, she went to the control room and handed Cherie a tape and a revised run of the show.

"This is all part of what I talked to you about yesterday. Load this up. When I give you the signal, put it on air and follow the storyboard on that sheet. Okay?"

Cherie held the tape and page in her hand, looking at Layne. "Okay. You got it."

"Thanks." She walked out and onto the set to be mic'd and have her earpiece adjusted. Settled behind the news desk, she braced for her countdown cue and for the red light of the camera to disappear. She had a moment of panic and thought this was crazy, but then she caught a glimpse of Deanna Mitchell standing in the back of the studio behind the camerapersons, and her determination was renewed.

She drew in a breath, straightened in her seat. Watched for her signal. The theme music played, the logo shot across the screen. Three. Two. One.

"Good morning. I'm Layne Davis and this is *The DC Morning Show.* We begin today with news out of Capitol Hill regarding the most recent push for a comprehensive women's rights bill. Our political reporter Della Bryant has the latest. Della..."

While the report was being broadcast, Layne checked her notes again. Barring karma, everything should go according to plan.

"Thank you for that, Della. This is the second time during this congressional session the bill has been brought to the floor. Advocates are hoping this time there will be some success. We turn now to the international front where the war continues to rage nearly a year since its start. Aid from around the world continues to pour in, but without direct intervention from the West, we may continue to talk about this assault for many more months to come. Simon Fields is on location with the latest. Simon…"

She got the signal in her ear that her guest had arrived and was coming up. Her heart thundered. She reached for the glass of water and took a long swallow.

"Thank you, Simon. We'll be right back after this short commercial break. Don't go anywhere."

Layne's pulse raced. She gave instruction to the production crew to bring out two chairs to the round table where she interviewed on-set guests. The techs got her settled at the circular table, checked her mic and gave the thumbs-up. Stacy darted on set to powder her nose and forehead seconds before Layne got her cue.

"Welcome back. As you all know, during this portion of the program, I have the privilege of bringing to the table a wide array of guests from politicians to reverends, CEOs to grassroots organizers and everyone in between. And while I have not been in this seat very long, I do hope that what I've brought to you is both entertaining and informative. Today is one of those days. I want to begin with this breaking news from the *Washington Post*." She gave a slight nod and the tape that she'd given Cherie bloomed big and bold on the screen: ALLEGATIONS OF CORPORATE MISCONDUCT AND WRONGFUL TERMINATIONS UNCOVERED AT WWDC NETWORK.

Because of the camera and studio lights on her, she could not see beyond the camera in front of her and the teleprompter, but she could clearly imagine the chaos and confusion in the control room. "It is not often or at all that you get to report on a place where you are employed. Sadly, that is what is happening here today. Based on the thorough investigative work of Brenda Walker and Lisbeth Grover at the *Post*, rumors and allegations that have been part of the culture here at WWDC have been brought to light. Pulitzer Prize–winning journalist Brenda Walker is my first guest this morning."

She knew that Cherie had her back and would cue the camerapersons as needed. Layne's last line on the storyboard sheet was: *Do not let Deanna stop you.*

The camera went to a two-shot to include Brenda Walker, who had joined Layne at the desk.

"Thank you so much for being here. As an investigative journalist myself, I know the hours of work and research involved and the level of verification required before releasing a story like this. Please tell us how it began and what you found out."

"Thank you for having me. If you recall, several months ago, we did a piece on Paul Waverly and his superstar arrival at WWDC. Less than a year into his arrival, he's gone. I found that to be curious. When we reached out to him we got no response and the station wouldn't return our calls. That only increased my desire to find out what had actually happened."

"And what did you find out?"

"The station has a pattern of dismissing male employees, who have in some way, at some point, worked for Deanna Mitchell. And they all signed NDAs."

She could almost hear the gasp in the control room. "NDAs?"

"Nondisclosure agreements. In other words, they are not supposed to talk about the details of their employment, termination or any compensations they may have received."

"What did you discover were the reasons for termination?"

"My research goes back five years, starting from when Deanna Mitchell took over as executive producer on daytime and evening news."

Layne swallowed. "How did you get around the NDAs?"

"To date, there are six terminations that I investigated. When I reached out to them and advised them they were not the only ones and that there was strength in numbers, they agreed to talk to me."

"And we have two of them with us today." Layne signaled and the screen filled with Brett Conway. "Thank you for being here with us today, Mr. Conway. As you all may remember, Brett Conway was the anchor prior to Paul Waverly. Mr. Conway, if you would tell us about your situation."

Brett explained how about a year into his hiring, Deanna Mitchell made innuendos alluding that a relationship with her could benefit him and his career. He was flattered at first, he said, and took her up on dinners and drinks after work. But there came a time when she became more aggressive and demanding. When he got uncomfortable and told Deanna as much, he started getting calls from Finance saying there were inconsistencies in his receipts, and there were anonymous complaints from tenants in the building where his apartment was leased by the network. Finally, he was suspended, then let go.

"I know this was not easy and that there are only so many details that you can share with us. I appreciate you being here, Mr. Conway."

"Of course."

The screen darkened and Layne turned to face the camera. "Now we have an in-studio guest that will join us."

The camera swung around to follow Paul Waverly as he walked toward the round table.

Her heart thundered. This was the nail in Deanna's coffin.

Paul walked onto the set, nodded to both women and sat down.

"Welcome…back, Mr. Waverly," Layne greeted. "I'm sure our audience is all too familiar with your presence on the screen, as you've greeted them every night in Charlotte and then every morning here in DC." She turned to the camera. "For anyone joining for the very first time, this is Paul Waverly, the anchor that replaced Brett Conway and who was then replaced by me. Thank you for being here, Mr. Waverly."

"I'm glad to be here."

"You agreed to work with Ms. Walker as part of her investigation into the allegations lodged against you. I understand that you did not sign an NDA but you have been suspended with the outcome more than likely to be your termination, like your predecessors."

"That's correct."

"Tell us as much as you feel comfortable about your experience here at WWDC."

Paul began with the day when he was approached by Deanna two years earlier, up to and including the emails, text messages, dinner alone in her office as well as her innuendos and his belief that much of her ire against him was Deanna's belief that he was involved with Layne.

"In the spirit of transparency," Layne cut in, "Paul and I have been seeing each other. For now that's a story for another day. Please continue."

"After I turned down her 'offer,' things changed."

"How?" Layne asked.

"She became overly critical. Countermanded everything I said. Essentially insinuated that I was off my game. And she continued to remind me that she'd gone to bat for me to come to WWDC. Then, I was suspended based on 'allegations' of improper behavior. I was out and you—" he looked to Layne "—were in."

Her expression tensed for a moment. "Thank you for being here today and sharing this disturbing account." She turned to face the camera. "Society has become accustomed to hearing that abusive behavior and retaliation only happens to women. But as you have heard today, that is no longer true." She closed the folder in front of her and faced the camera. "Next up, Kevin Parker is at the site of the grand opening of the community center spearheaded by real estate mogul Montgomery Grant, right after this commercial break."

The instant the cameras were off Deanna came flying across the studio floor and up in the face of Layne. Her face was red with fury. "What do you think you're doing? You think you can smear me like this and get away with it? I'll have your job and you'll never work in broadcasting again."

Layne leaned back and smiled with satisfaction. "I rest my case," she said softly.

Within moments Security was on the floor, ushering a ranting Deanna away.

The fallout from the interview was swift. There was an emergency meeting of the board to launch an internal investigation and the PR team was in damage control mode.

Layne was called into the office of the network president, Gabe Fitzpatrick.

She entered his corner office on the top floor. She'd been at the station for three-going-on-four years and this was the first time she'd actually been in the same room with Gabriel Fitzpatrick. He was imposing, to say the least, with his expensive suit, thick shock of snow-white hair and piercing blue eyes, his well-over-six-foot frame and the physique of an athlete.

"Please come in and have a seat, Ms. Davis," he instructed in a melodious baritone.

Layne lifted her chin and crossed the threshold.

"Drink?" he asked, walking over to a built-in bar

on the far wall. He poured a short shot of bourbon in a beveled glass.

"No. Thank you."

"Have a seat."

He walked back to his chair and she took a seat opposite his massive desk.

"What you did today...has caused a great deal of problems for this network, of which I am president." He took a swallow of his drink. His cheeks reddened. "But it is a problem we will deal with. If these accusations against Deanna are true—" he rocked his square jaw "—she will be dealt with as well. And I can assure you that there will be no reprisals against you. That's not the kind of organization I want to run or represent." He finished off his drink and set down his glass. "The board will be meeting later today and we'll issue a statement."

She licked her dry lips and nodded.

"It took a lot of guts to do what you did on live television." He almost smiled. "A real journalist."

"I'll take that as a compliment."

"It is." He stood and so did Layne.

"Thank you for seeing me and for your support. But I'll be handing in my resignation."

Gabriel didn't respond.

Layne turned and walked out and realized that she was shaking all over.

For the next week, every newspaper, news outlet and cable station led off with the scandal at WWDC and reshaped the conversation around the power dynamics in the workplace.

* * *

"Looks like we might have started something," Paul said as they lay next to each other on Layne's bed, reading the Sunday paper.

"I've stopped taking calls for interviews," Layne replied. "I'll let the powers that be duke it out."

"Same here." He turned on his side to face her. "Know what I really want to do?"

"What?"

"Get away. A real vacation. Away from all the noise."

She smiled slowly. "Oh, really? Like go on the lam."

Paul chuckled. "We're not fugitives. But seriously, away from the calls, the demands—just relax, re-group, make love." He stroked her hip. "And plan for our wedding."

She blinked. "Our wedding?"

"Yeah. I love you, woman, and I know damned well that you love me. We've put our lives on hold for too long, and that diamond I got you four years ago has burned several holes in my pocket."

She covered her mouth with her hand. "What? You still have the ring? You didn't sell it?"

He rose up on his elbow so that he could look in her eyes. "I couldn't. Might sound crazy but as hurt and pissed off as I was, there was this part of me that wanted to believe that we'd find our way back to each other."

Layne sniffed back tears. She cupped his cheek. "I love you," she whispered. "Let's do this, for real and for always." She leaned in and kissed him tenderly, the way her heart felt toward this stubborn, smart, handsome, sexy, loving man. And he was all hers.

Layne and Paul ducked out of the spotlight for six glorious weeks. They rented a bungalow in Hawaii for two weeks, learned how to surf, then jetted off to Belize where they toured, ate, danced, drank late into the evening and made love until the sun came up.

She had never been so happy, so full, than she had these past six weeks. It was like a pre-honeymoon, and she asked Paul what he planned for an encore.

"That," he said, "is a surprise. Keep that passport ready."

"Can't I get a hint?" she asked, kissing his bare chest before straddling his naked body.

"That would take the fun out of the surprise." He lifted his head and teased her nipple with his tongue.

She trembled ever so slightly, pressed her palms against his chest and rose up to position herself above his rising erection before easing all the way down. She felt him lengthen and stiffen inside her. She moaned. Her lids drifted closed and she held her bottom lip between her teeth as she began to move up and down along his length, sending shockwaves through them both.

As the maid of honor, Tina made all the arrangements with the management of Essex House to host the wedding, and of course she arranged to have the *Post*'s Style and Entertainment writer cover the nuptials. Layne would have been fine with a small ceremony, but her bestie wouldn't hear of it. "You'll only walk down that aisle once—hopefully—" she'd said, "so we are going to make it a walk to remember."

Actually, Layne was totally grateful that Tina had taken control of all the details for her big day. All she had to concentrate on was what her new life would be with Paul, and decorating the house they'd purchased in Georgetown upon their return from their getaway. They intended to move into it after their honeymoon—destination still unknown to Layne.

In between fittings for her dress and furniture shopping, she got news that her segment that outed the underbelly of WWDC had been nominated for a Daytime Emmy, and both she and Paul were in the running for excellence in journalism.

The past year had been fraught with obstacles for her and Paul, ones they'd created between themselves and those created outside of them. But what peeled that all away was above all else their love for each other. They recognized their faults and weaknesses and loved each other anyway, because together they made each other stronger and better.

As the doors to the grand ballroom of Essex House opened and the strains of the wedding march played, by a trio of violinists, rose sweetly to the rafters, Layne's heart soared at the magic that greeted her.

The 100-plus guests rose to their feet as Layne walked the rose-petaled aisle toward her future. The look of love and adoration in Paul's eyes guided her steps and when she took his hand and accepted his band of love, they vowed they would spend every day of their life together better than the day before.

The reception was one for the ages. A full band kept the guests on their feet, and the incredible menu, overseen by Alonzo Grant himself, was photographed as much as the bride and groom.

Whether they wanted to be or not, Layne and Paul Waverly were celebrities and reporters wanted to capture every moment.

The party went on to near midnight. Layne and Paul were exhausted but overwhelmed with happiness. As the party began to wind down and the music slowed, Paul danced with his bride.

"You are absolutely beautiful," he whispered in her ear. "And I love you more than I can ever express. We're going to have the best life possible. I promise you that."

"I'm ready to start my honeymoon," she whispered, looking up into his eyes, "and our new life together."

"My brother's advice is happy wife, happy life. Your wish is my command, my love." He grinned and kissed the tip of her nose.

"And I do believe that no one will miss us if we sneak off to our honeymoon suite upstairs. Tina will take care of everything."

"I like the sound of that." He took a quick look around. "Let's go." He took her hand and they snuck out of the ballroom and headed in the direction of the private elevator, when they were stopped halfway by a short, stocky man in a dark suit.

"I don't want to impose on your special day." He pulled a card out of the breast pocket of his jacket and held it out. "My name is Evan Miles. I'm—"

Layne and Paul cut him off at the same time. "I know who you are," they said in unison.

"Head of MSCBS," Paul offered.

Evan chuckled. "I'll make this brief. Please call me at your earliest. I have an offer that I think you'll like." He smiled from one to the other. Paul took the card. "Congratulations." The man gave a short nod of his head, turned and walked away.

Paul and Layne looked at each other. He tucked the card in his pocket. Layne pressed the button for the elevator.

"Wonder what he wants?" Layne said as they stepped on the elevator and the door slid closed.

Paul turned her toward him and pressed her against the wall of the elevator. "Frankly, my dear, I don't give a damn," he said in a really bad imitation of Clark Gable.

Layne sputtered a laugh. "Neither do I," she said, linking her arms around his neck for a kiss that lasted all the way to the penthouse floor.

Six months later

"Welcome to *Roundtable in the Morning* with Layne Davis."

"And her other half, Paul Waverly," Paul said. "We're here at the studio in Washington, DC, and we have a dynamic lineup for you this morning."

"Congressman Abrams, head of the Congressional Black Caucus, is here to talk about the efforts being made to push through the Voting Rights Act," Layne said.

"I'm looking forward to talking to him and really hearing why are there so many in Congress that continue to fight against it. And later in the hour we'll be talking with *New York Times* bestselling author Celeste Graham, who'll be discussing her book *Unraveled*, a behind-the-scenes look at what happens to a country when everyone is under surveillance."

"Scary stuff and a little too close to what is becoming a reality."

Paul nodded in agreement. "Stay where you are. Right after this break, we'll be talking with Congressman Abrams."

When they'd returned from their honeymoon in Maui and settled into their new home, Paul had come across the card from Evan Miles.

"Hey, babe," he'd said, walking into the kitchen where Layne was flipping bacon strips in the frying pan.

"Hmm," she'd said and begun placing the bacon on a plate with a paper towel.

"We never called Evan Miles."

She placed the tray of bacon and toast on the table and spooned scrambled eggs onto the tray. She sat down. "True. Do you want to?" she'd asked.

He'd shrugged. "We should at least see what he has to say."

She studied him for a moment and smiled. "Getting that itch again?"

He snorted a laugh. "Like you aren't. I see how you devour every bit of news and offer your analysis of every newscaster on television."

"Humph." She feigned offense. "And?"

"Can't hurt to see what he has to say."

She brought a slice of bacon to her mouth and crunched it between her teeth. She chewed slowly. An easy smile lifted her lush mouth. "Can't hurt," she agreed.

So they'd called. Two months after their honeymoon, they'd met with Evan Miles, who offered them the deal of a lifetime. In the infamous words of *The Godfather*, it was an offer they couldn't refuse. They would have their own show, control over content and approval of all guests, covering everything from politics to entertainment. They would be the network's competition to *Morning Joe* featuring Joe and Mika—who, like Paul and Layne, had met through work and married.

Layne and Paul were magical together and quickly became the newest broadcasting darlings. When they sat in the corporate offices of MSCBS to sign their contract, they knew that they were embarking on their next journey together and vowed to be partners for life on-screen and off.

* * * * *